Jobyna's Blues

Also by Jane Alden

Across A Crowded Room

Jobyna's Blues

Jane Alden

Desert Palm Press

Jobyna's Blues

by Jane Alden

© 2019 by Jane Alden

ISBN (book): 9781948327381
ISBN (epub): 9781948327398
ISBN (pdf): 9781948327404

Desert Palm Press
1961 Main Street, Suite 220
Watsonville, California 95076
www.desertpalmpress.com

Editor: Heather Flournoy
Cover Design: TreeHouse Studio

Printed in the United States of America
First Edition June 2019

ACKNOWLEDGEMENTS

Jobyna's Blues started, by another name, as a story about a folk singer who becomes involved with an English pop singer in the halcyon days of the early 1960s. Jobyna and Lily showed up, took over the narrative, and steered things back to 1924 and wouldn't let go. They wanted to tell how women performers, especially women of color, paved the way for their sisters who came after.

Having been born and raised in the south, I felt I could write authentically about their travels through Tennessee, Mississippi, Louisiana, and Alabama, but I'm forever grateful for the generous support and careful reading and commentary of diverse beta readers whom I contacted through Golden Crown Literary Society. They set me straight on several plot and culture points.

Members of my writers' group provided inspiration and helpful criticism along the way, and my partner encouraged me to question assumptions and avoid clichés. She was always ready to make time to let me read parts aloud, an exercise that never fails to sharpen things up.

Lee Fitzsimmons at Desert Palm Press provides just the right touch of support and collaborative encouragement to me and I suspect to all the authors at DPP. Heather Flournoy has many wonderful attributes as an editor. Most importantly, she's kind. What an honor to have a cover by Ann McMan.

PROLOGUE

2004

LILY FELT THE SUN warm on her eyelids, before she was fully awake. She always asked the night aide to leave the venetian blinds open so that the morning light would wake her.

"Aren't you afraid of Peeping Toms?" The young man liked to tease her, thinking she enjoyed it. She didn't.

"No, honey. I'm long past being peeped at." She bantered with the aide to be polite, but she didn't like him much. He halfway did his job, trying to get by with as little effort as possible. Still, it was best to stay on people's good side at Shady Rest.

Her favorite one was Sondra, a candy striper who came in to wake her every weekday morning. Sondra had spunk. She also had a ring in her nose. Lily wanted the sun to wake her so she wouldn't miss any of Sondra's quick, early morning visits. Lily heard the swish of the red-and-white striped starched cotton apron Sondra always wore and opened her eyes.

"Good morning, Miz Lily," Sondra said. "You already awake? I don't wonder because you must be excited. Today is a very special day, isn't it? Your ninety-seventh birthday."

Sondra lifted Lily up to lean against the headboard of her single bed and stuffed two pillows behind her back. "You got to eat more, Miz Lily. I can feel every knob in your backbone. Wish I had that problem. Look at these thighs. Do you want to go to the dining room for breakfast this morning or do you want me to spoil you with breakfast in bed for your birthday?"

"I want to eat here if you'll sit with me and talk. You always run off too fast." Lily heard the whiny tone in her voice. "If you have time, that is." She really could use Sondra's company this morning. She was feeling a little down in the dumps. Sondra brought what often was the only bright spot in Lily's day. Precious few of the other residents at Shady Rest had enough of their marbles left to be any kind of company at all.

"Let me go tell Mrs. Posey that you and me are going to have a nice long visit this morning to celebrate. I'll be right back with your breakfast and some coffee for me." She patted Lily's face. This was one of the things Lily liked about Sondra—she wasn't afraid to touch her.

Sondra came back carrying a breakfast tray, settled it on Lily's lap, and pulled a chair up close to the bed. "I got oatmeal for you. I think that's one of your favorites. It's the made kind this morning for a change, not the instant kind. Do you want me to help you fix it?" Sondra sprinkled the hot cereal with sugar, added a pat of butter, and covered it all with milk.

Lily noticed the blue tint of the milk. They served only that awful skim stuff in the nursing home. She thought it foolish to limit all these old people's fat intake. What difference could it make at this point? "Aren't you going to have some breakfast, too?"

"No, Miz Lily. I told you, I need to lose me some weight." Sondra smoothed the apron over her ample lap.

"I think you look just fine. You remind me of someone very special to me a long time ago."

Sondra picked up one of the framed photographs from Lily's bedside table. She turned the picture around and held it close to Lily's face. "Who's this?"

Lily squinted at the old picture of eight young black women lined up on a stage, their long legs bare and their midriffs covered by huge ostrich feather fans. "That's me. The second from the left."

"You were a dancer?" Sondra's eyes grew big, looking back and forth between the photograph and Lily's face.

"It was a long time ago, child. That picture was taken in 1924. Truth be told, I never was much of a dancer, no matter how hard my cousin Ruth tried to teach me. That's her on the end."

"Is one of these the girl I remind you of?" Sondra brought the picture close to her own face.

"No, honey. You remind me of the star of the show back then, Jobyna Jones. Do you know who she was?"

Sondra nodded. "Wasn't she a singer? I read about her. Is that the way you say it? Jobyna? I was never sure."

Lily smiled. "Yes. She always said, 'Rhymes with Carolina.' When I knew her, though, she was already so famous that no one had to ask how to say her name. Empress of the Blues, they called her. And us dancers, we were the Tennessee Toe-Tappers. We traveled all over the South, Memphis and New Orleans and Nashville. Back then, black folks had their own theaters. White folks couldn't come except on special nights. When they did, they had to sit in the balcony. But they came every time they could just to hear Jobyna sing the blues. She was a big, pretty girl like you, and she had the most beautiful voice you ever heard. Like an angel."

Lily settled back against her pillows and closed her eyes. She could hear Jobyna singing when things were still and quiet like this. It seemed the older she got the easier it was to call up Jobyna's voice in her memory.

"Miz Lily, are you asleep? Do you want me to take this tray away?"

"No, honey, I'm not sleeping. I'm just remembering."

"You should write a book, Miz Lily. Just think of the things you've seen. Or you could tell it to me, and I'll write it down."

"Oh, honey, I've always been more likely to read books than write them, until my eyes got so bad." Lily saw an opportunity to encourage Sondra's spending time with her. "But we'll see."

"When my mama says, 'We'll see,' it usually means 'No way.'"

Lily laughed. "I wouldn't dare tell most of it, even though almost all of them must be gone now."

Sondra held up another framed picture, this one a more contemporary photo of a young woman perched on a stool playing a guitar and highlighted by a spotlight. Her dark hair was long and straight, parted in the middle, the reflected light creating a halo effect. "And who's this, Miz Lily?"

"That's my granddaughter. Her name's Jobyna, too, named after the original, but she calls herself Jobie." Lily took the picture from Sondra and ran her finger gently across it. "Her mother was my daughter, my only child. She died when Jobie was born, and my husband and I raised her like our own. Jobie was a singer, too, used to be. Now she's an artist, in New York City."

Lily looked up at Sondra. "The Bible says, 'Pride goeth before a fall,' but I don't believe they were saying I can't be proud of my Jobie, do you?"

Sondra patted her hand. "No'm, I'm sure that's not what the Bible means."

A middle-aged woman in a pink polyester aide's uniform bustled in the door. "Are you done with your breakfast, sweetheart? I need Sondra to come help me pass morning meds."

Lily didn't like most of the help, but she flat hated this woman, the pushy and disrespectful Mrs. Posey, the Aide Supervisor. Lily especially despised that the woman called her "sweetheart." It was too familiar and condescending, and she suspected she called everyone by pet names because it was too much trouble to remember what their real names were.

Sondra picked up breakfast tray. "I'm sorry. Are you done?" Lily nodded.

Sondra turned on her way out the door. "I'll come back at the end of my shift, okay? Maybe we can start writing your book."

"We'll see, honey. Pull the door to on your way out, please."

"Yes'm." Sondra paused again on the threshold. "Happy birthday, Miz Lily."

Lily settled back on her pillows and closed her eyes again. Her thoughts drifted back to 1924, the first time she laid eyes on Jobyna Jones.

PART ONE

1924

LILY

Chapter One

LILY WASN'T SURE BEING there was a good idea. She could change her mind now, turn and walk out of the apartment house through the big double front doors the way she came in. She wouldn't have to talk to Jobyna Jones, the famous blues singer, let alone try out in her living room for the chorus line in her traveling show.

Ruth gave Lily a push from behind. "Don't embarrass me by backing out now. She's doing me a big favor because my mama used to be her dresser. If you really want to get out of Chattanooga, like you say a thousand times a day, now's your chance to get your nose out of a book and start living your life."

Lily bit the inside of her cheek. "But I don't have any talent. I can't sing, that's for sure."

"All the talent you need is in your looks. Do you ever look at yourself in the mirror? They want light-skinned girls like you for the chorus. You've always had good hair." Ruth reached to smooth a stray curl at Lily's forehead. "Besides, how hard do you think it is to dance in a line with seven other girls and practically no clothes on? You can shuffle from foot to foot, right? If Jobyna likes your looks, you're in." Ruth put her hand on the small of Lily's back and pushed again. "Just get up the stairs."

Lily hung back and let Ruth knock on the door of Apartment 202. Both girls jumped as the door jerked open. A small, fierce-looking man with a wiry goatee and eyes that glowed with alert anger glared at the women. He held the door only halfway open with his left hand and blocked the doorway with his body. Lily watched his right hand go to his waistband behind his back. *Is he reaching for a gun?*

Ruth took a step back, bumping into Lily. "Little T, it's me, Ruth. Remember, I was supposed to bring my cousin Lily around to see Jobyna?"

The man straightened the lapels of his pinstriped suit jacket. He opened the door wider, stepped back to let the two girls in and gestured toward an open door across the living room. "She's in the bedroom."

This time even Ruth, who was never one to be shy, hesitated. "Do you want us to go on in there?" She touched Lily's arm. Lily couldn't tell whether the touch was for support or to hold her back.

"Go on." He slammed the door and shot the lock bolt into place.

Ruth gave Lily's arm a tug. The two young women crossed the living room to stand in the doorway of the bedroom. The room was almost bare, more impersonal than a hotel room would be. Lily reasoned that the apartment must be a temporary stopover for Jobyna between tour dates. The floral pattern on the wallpaper was faded to a blurry beige, and the rug that covered the middle of the floor was clean but worn thin in places. A plain maple bureau and dressing table had nothing on them—no makeup, powder, pictures. Nothing.

Jobyna was a spot of color in the otherwise drab room. She was propped against the headboard with a notebook in her lap, wearing a scarlet silk dressing gown and turban. As Lily gazed at her, the rest of the room and Ruth disappeared. There was a circle drawn around Jobyna, in sharp focus, with everything else fuzzy and blotted out.

She looked younger and softer than Lily expected. When Jobyna looked up from the notebook in her lap, Lily saw sadness or fatigue in her eyes.

Her eyebrows went up when she saw Lily. "Who you got here, Ruth?"

"This is Lily, my cousin I told you about, Jobyna. You know Gladys is leaving the show because of her baby coming, and Lily is a real good dancer. You can see she has the looks. She'd love to go on the road with us. You remember, you said I could bring her by."

Jobyna smiled. "Uh-huh. So, you're a dancer, baby?"

Ruth jumped in before Lily could answer. "I've been showing her some steps. She catches on real fast."

"Where you from, Lily?"

"I was raised in Jasper, but now I stay here, in Chattanooga, with my sister."

"What does your mama say about you going with my show?"

"My mama passed." Lily felt a catch in her throat. She was afraid she might start to cry from nervousness. She balled her fists behind her back and dug her fingernails into her palms.

"How old are you?"

Ruth had coached Lily to be ready for this question. Lily was surprised by how easily the lie came out of her mouth. "Eighteen."

Jobyna smiled and nodded. "Eighteen. Uh-huh. Turn around, Lily."

Lily turned halfway around to face the open bedroom door. Across the living room, she could see the man still standing guard by the front door. He scowled at her. Lily closed her eyes tightly to keep from fidgeting under Jobyna's gaze.

"Little T, she's going to come by the theater this afternoon. Tell Max."

"Tell him what?"

"Tell him she's going to try out for the chorus, what do you think?"

Lily glanced back over her shoulder at Jobyna for some sign of what she was expected to do next, but Jobyna's attention had already gone back to the notebook. Reading upside down, Lily could tell that she was writing poetry or lyrics to a song. "Thank you, Miss Jones. I promise you won't regret this."

"Call me Jobyna, baby," she said without looking up. "Don't let her get lost on the way, Ruth."

"Oh, I won't, Jobyna." Ruth grabbed Lily's hand and pulled her across the living room and out the front door. It slammed behind them.

"Who was that man? Why is he guarding Jobyna? Do you think he had a gun?"

"Oh, that's Little T. He's just trying to make himself useful and important. Stay out of his way and you'll be fine. Never mind him, what about Jobyna? Isn't she amazing?"

"She's beautiful, but why is she so sad?"

"She's happy when she's on the stage. Wait till you see her sing in front of an audience. Someday I'm going to be a singer just like her." She grabbed Lily's hand again. "Let's get out of here."

Chapter Two

ON THE SIDEWALK IN front of the Chattanooga Tivoli Theatre, Lily paced back and forth between the two glass-framed posters on either side of the fancy box office. She stopped to read the poster again—*Jobyna Jones, Empress of The Blues, Live On Stage Tonight With The Fletcher Henderson Orchestra Featuring Louis Armstrong.* She checked her reflection in the poster glass, smoothed her hair, and straightened the slim skirt of her cotton dress. She walked out to the busy street and glanced up and down it for Ruth. Even though the sun hadn't set, the thousand lights that surrounded the theater's red, black, and white marquee were lit and chasing each other around the ten-foot-tall letters that spelled out TIVOLI.

Lily heard the clicking of tap shoes from the side of the building. Ruth appeared around the corner. "Where you been, girl? I've been waiting for you. I thought you backed out. Remember, Jobyna told me to not let you get lost." Ruth wore a black leotard with a brightly colored scarf tied around her hips. She eyed Lily's dress and shoes. "We have to get you in some rehearsal clothes. Come on, girl. Performers don't go in the public entrance. The stage door is around here."

Lily liked the sound of the word "performers," but she was far from sure that would apply to her.

The stage door off the alley opened into a narrow, dim passageway. Lily could smell a mixture of floor wax, cigarette smoke, and a smell new to her which she thought must be greasepaint makeup. Ruth led her backstage, up an iron staircase and across a catwalk open on the right to the stage below and lined on the left with dressing room doors. As they passed a closed door, they heard Jobyna's raised voice.

"You hear me good, Charlie. Our deal is ten cents a seat. Every night we've been here we've played to a full house. That means seventeen hundred and fifty asses every night in seats. That's one hundred and seventy-five dollars every night. Our deal is already less than the owner pays white acts. I won't sit still to be cheated out of what we agreed to. So you go tell him."

"Jobyna—"

"I mean it," Jobyna yelled. Lily and Ruth jumped as something glass hit the inside of the door and shattered.

A man threw the door open and ducked another flying bottle that smashed against the walkway's iron railing. He slammed the door. When he saw the two girls, he smiled and hitched his pants up and straightened his lapels. "A small disagreement. Not even out of the ordinary. Nothing to worry about."

He extended his hand to Lily. "Charlie Reed, Chief Booker of T-O-B-A." When neither girl responded, he went on. "Theater Owners Booking Association. We decide which acts go on where and for how much." He thrust his chest out and glanced again at the closed door to Jobyna's dressing room. "We represent Jobyna in all her tours. And you pretty ladies are?" He still held Lily's hand, and though he included Ruth in his compliment, he focused his attention on Lily.

"We're in Jobyna's show," Ruth said. She pulled Lily away from Charlie and headed down the corridor. She said under her breath, "Trying to be a big shot. T-O-B-A. Jobyna says that stands for Tough on Black Asses."

Lily grinned at Jobyna's joke. She was impressed that Jobyna stood up for herself with Charlie Reed.

Ruth steered Lily into a cramped communal dressing room at the end of the corridor where seven other women were pulling on leotards, putting on makeup in front of mirrors, lacing up tap shoes, or standing around in various stages of undress laughing, smoking, and chattering to each other.

Ruth chuckled when she saw Lily's big-eyed look. "This is only rehearsal. When you get in the show, just get used to things being really crazy before performances."

Lily noticed that when Ruth called her a performer, she optimistically said "when" not "if" she was in the show. She still wasn't so sure herself.

"Don't stand there with your mouth hanging open. They'll all think you're from the country."

"I am."

"I know that, but they don't have to. Let me find you some tights and some shoes."

Jobyna's dancers clattered down the stairway, with Ruth leading Lily behind them. The unfamiliar tap shoes made Lily's feet almost slip out from under her on the metal stair treads. She could hear tinny piano music coming from the stage, playing a number that Ruth had made her practice dance steps to. On stage, the dancers began to line up.

Ruth pulled the neckline of Lily's leotard down to show a little more cleavage. "You look good, girl. That's Max, the director. I'm going to tell him that Jobyna wants you to try out today and go with us to Nashville tomorrow. Wait here. Let me do the talking."

Lily watched Ruth speak to the director and point toward her standing in the wings. Max shook his head and scowled in her direction. He stepped over to the edge of the stage to speak to someone sitting in the dark beyond the footlights. Lily closed her eyes and took a deep breath to calm herself.

When she opened her eyes, Max was standing in front of her with his hands on his hips. "Little T says I'm supposed to try you out for the chorus. Which means that, with your looks, if you can at least walk and chew gum at the same time, you're in, but I've still got to make you into what passes for a dancer. Get in line with the other girls and try to keep up."

She stood behind Ruth and next to the obviously pregnant Gladys, the girl she was going to replace—if she was lucky. By matching their steps, Lily managed to get through the rehearsal. She felt her insides vibrating with a mix of anxiety and excitement. *Is Jobyna here somewhere?* Lily peered into the gloom beyond the footlights. *She might be watching me right now. Who will decide if I can join the show? Max or Little T or Jobyna herself?*

The piano sounded the last chord in the last run-through of rehearsal. Max clapped his hands and pointed his finger at each of the chorus girls. "Tonight is our last show in Chattanooga. We leave for Nashville early tomorrow morning. Show up on time and sober, and don't bring any Johnnys around the train. Get your goodbyes all out of the way tonight."

The girls scattered in groups of twos and threes. Their tap shoes made a clatter on the hardwood stage that added to the chatter of their voices. Ruth grabbed Lily's hand and pulled her backstage.

"Does that mean I'm going on the tour?"

"I think so. Did you see the size of Gladys' belly? This is surely her last show, then you'll take her place in Nashville. Let's not ask too many questions. I think because you managed to get through the tryout without falling down, you're in. Besides, I don't see anybody else waiting in the wings. We need to go and find a costume to fit you." Ruth hurried her along. Lily squinted into the stage lights, trying to make out whether Jobyna was there watching.

Chapter Three

LILY STOOD IN THE middle of the main waiting room of Chattanooga Terminal Train Station. She clutched her battered cardboard suitcase, borrowed from her sister, and gazed up at the ceiling dome topped with a skylight in the center. Ruth grabbed her hand to hustle her along toward the passenger gates.

"Come on, girl. I swear, I don't know where your head is at most of the time. It seems like I'm having to yank you by the hand everywhere we go. We have to find Jobyna's railroad car if we don't want to be left behind."

"Ruth, you're older than me and you certainly know more than I do. Are you going to get sick of having to lead me around?"

"Maybe. But I'll tell you if I do. Right now, we have to hurry."

"I know. I'm just trying to memorize everything so I never forget this moment as long as I live."

Ruth stopped an official-looking man in a dark-blue uniform and asked directions to the railroad sidetrack number written on the crumpled piece of paper she pulled from her coat pocket.

"He says it's this way." Ruth jerked Lily along again. They dodged the incoming flow of passengers eagerly rushing to find family and friends or to catch taxis for the next leg of their journeys.

Ruth checked the paper again. "This is the way." They took the last flight of stairs to the right and emerged on a platform next to a Pullman sleeper painted bright red with ten-foot-tall yellow letters: *The Empress of Blues—Jobyna Jones And the Tennessee Toe-Tappers Revue.* Chorus girls were climbing the metal steps at the front of the car. Red caps were rushing back and forth like ants, loading crates of scenery, props, and costumes in a freight car behind.

"Come on." Ruth grabbed the handle of Lily's suitcase. "I told you you'd make us late."

Ruth led Lily down the narrow aisle of the dormitory-style sleeping area. Bunks stacked three high were curtained off with navy-blue velvet drapes. Ruth and Lily threw their suitcases on two bottom bunks across from each other.

"Oh, no, New Girl." A chorus girl with legs that seemed to go all the way to her waist stepped in front of Lily. "You're on the top bunk here over the wheels." She grabbed Lily's suitcase and flung it onto said bunk and stood with her hands on her hips, challenging Lily to differ.

Ruth stepped forward to argue. "Listen, Hattie. Who died and made you the boss?"

Lily placed a hand on Ruth's arm. "It's fine."

"Come on, Lily. Let's go look at the rest of the car." Ruth turned her nose up in Hattie's direction. "She's just jealous of your looks," Ruth whispered as they squeezed sideways past other girls moving along the narrow corridor between the bunks.

They passed a tiny lavatory. Lily stuck her head inside. "Are all of us supposed to use that?"

"Yes, so it's best to wake up early and get in ahead of everyone else. That's not too hard. These girls are lazy."

Beyond a partition, the car opened up into a coach area with walnut paneling and benches upholstered in damask fabric. Past the bench seating section were dining tables. Beyond that was a compact kitchen.

"Fancy," Lily said.

Ruth nodded. "Just wait till you see Jobyna's rooms." She led the way back to a door past the kitchen. An etched glass window in the door was covered by red velvet drapes. Ruth tested the doorknob and pushed it open. They stepped into a private lounge area with a bedroom beyond.

Lily turned in a slow circle. "Look how different this is from that apartment in Chattanooga." A huge crystal chandelier hung in the middle of the car over leather chairs and sofas and a damask chaise lounge. Art deco wall sconces cast cones of light on a ceiling covered with a mural of dark-skinned, fat cherubs reclining on clouds strumming harps. A bar ran along one side, stocked with liquor in crystal decanters. Through the open bedroom door, Lily could see an oversized bed covered in a mink spread.

"Are we supposed to be in here?" Lily started back toward the door.

"Don't worry, she's not here yet. She gets on at the last minute after the car's been hooked up to the rest of the train." No sooner had she spoken than the train backed into the coupling of Jobyna's car, causing Ruth and Lily to lurch forward onto the chaise lounge. Before they could scramble to their feet, the door opened. Jobyna stood in the doorway, her substantial body wrapped in a fur coat, a matching turban covering her hair.

Ruth found her voice first. "Jobyna, I was just showing Lily around, and we got lost."

"Lost. On a seventy-foot-long railroad car." Jobyna took off her coat and turban and handed them to Lily. "Put these on the bed, baby." Underneath, she wore a canary-yellow silk dressing gown. Her hair was done up with bobby pins in tight pin curls.

"I don't mind you showing off some to your pretty friend. I'm proud of my train car, too. Lord knows I've worked hard enough for all this, and I pay enough to keep it going. It sure beats sneaking in the back door of some broke-down third-rate boarding house in these cracker towns we tour."

Jobyna kicked off her shoes and reclined on the chaise with a sigh. "Pour me a drink since you're here and pour one for yourself and Lily. I can use some company. That's your name, right? Lily, isn't it?"

"Yes, ma'am."

Jobyna took the glass from Ruth. "Well, sit down." She motioned toward the leather chairs.

Ruth handed Lily a crystal glass filled with amber liquid halfway to the top and shot her a look that said, *Sit down and don't say nothin'.*

Lily brought the glass up to her lips and peeked over the rim toward Jobyna lying on the chaise. She saw a difference in Jobyna's eyes from the first time they'd met in the apartment in Chattanooga. The sadness and fatigue were gone. *This is her real home. She's happiest when she's on the road.*

As she tipped up the glass to drink, she made the mistake of trying to breathe at the same time. The fumes sent a spasm through her throat, starting her coughing and sputtering.

Ruth looked on in horror.

"Get her some water, Ruth," Jobyna said.

Once Lily got herself under control, she said, "I'm sorry. It tastes different than it looks."

Jobyna shook her head and chuckled. "How old are you really, baby?"

Lily glanced at Ruth. "Seventeen."

"Seventeen how long?"

"Just turned."

"That's what I thought. You said you live with your sister. Does she know you're coming with us?"

This was the moment of opportunity for Lily. She was about to start

19

on a new chapter in her life, away from the farm in Chattanooga. She could live in a world that she had only read about in library books, the heroine of an exciting story starring herself and this fascinating woman. Lily locked eyes with Jobyna. "My sister has her own family. I'll be one less mouth to feed, and I'm going to send her money when I get paid."

Jobyna patted the side of the chaise. "Come here, baby." She scooted over to give Lily some room beside her. "If you're going to send your sister money, you don't need to be learning how to drink liquor." She took the glass and gently brushed the back of her hand across Lily's cheek.

The train jerked forward, then stopped, then began to roll out of the station with a grinding sound of metal wheels against the rails. "Go on back up front, girls, and I'll see you in Nashville."

Ruth and Lily hustled to the door.

"And Ruth, send Hattie back here."

"Yes'm."

Chapter Four

LILY SAT SQUEEZED INTO the corner of the dressing room in the Nashville Bijou Theater, staying out of the way of the madhouse atmosphere that swirled around the one long makeup mirror. The entire chorus line was trying to apply makeup and do their hair at the same time. The air was blue with cigarette smoke and rough language.

Lily was dressed in her costume and make up, having been the first into the backstage dressing room. As soon as the railroad car pulled into the Nashville train station, she urged Ruth off the train, through the station, and over to a line of waiting taxis for the ride to the theater. She wanted to have as much time for makeup, hair, and costume as possible. She had enough to worry about with trying to pull off the dance routine. She didn't want to worry about being rushed dressing.

In the middle of all the racket, the dressing room door flew open with a loud bang, making all the girls jump and turn toward the noise. Little T stood in the doorway with his hands in the pockets of his pinstriped pants. Lily recognized the scowl she first saw in Jobyna's Chattanooga apartment. He looked around the room, then walked straight over to where Hattie sat, her elbow on the makeup table and a cigarette hanging from her lips.

Little T took Hattie's chin in his hand and raised her face to meet his fierce gaze. When he spoke, it wasn't only to Hattie, but to the whole room. "You gals remember what I told you about smiling while you're up there on that stage, you hear? I catch you looking bored or less than absolutely joyful to be dancing for all those customers out front, and I'll fine you, just like always." He moved away from Hattie and strutted around the room, checking each girl's makeup and hair. He paused in front of Lily in the corner. "You got that, New Girl?"

Little T was close enough that Lily could smell his bay-rum-scented shaving lotion. He wore a vest with a gold pocket watch chain that Lily had seen in photographs of rich men. Hanging from the chain and staring at Lily with ruby eyes was a gold lion's head. A diamond the size of a lima bean glittered in its open mouth. Lily nodded her head and held her breath. With one more scowling look around the room, Little T walked out and slammed the door.

Lily whispered to Ruth. "How did he get here? He wasn't on the train, was he?"

"No, he drives the bus with the band between shows."

Hattie overheard the two women. She turned back to the mirror, stubbed out her cigarette, and began to apply bright red lipstick. "He calls himself her manager. Manager." She sniffed. "He can't even manage himself. All he knows how to do is count money and ask Jobyna to buy him more of those three-hundred-dollar suits he wears." Nervous giggles erupted around the room.

"You better be careful with talk like that, Hattie. If Jobyna hears you, she'll knock you down for sure," Ruth said.

"I can handle Jobyna," Hattie said. She caught Lily's eye in the mirror's reflection and gave her a smirk.

What does that look mean, and what does Hattie mean to Jobyna?

***

Standing behind the heavy, maroon velvet curtains of the Bijou Theater stage, Lily listened to the overflow crowd of sixteen hundred customers chant Jobyna's name. Every seat in the auditorium, including the balcony, was occupied. An eight-piece backing band took the stage. Max wrangled the dancers into line for their entrance. Lily's heart was beating so hard that she looked down to see if the audience would be able to notice her chest thudding. She suppressed a sudden need for the bathroom.

The drummer counted off eight beats and the band struck up a hot jazz number. The curtains opened, and the girl behind Lily bumped into her, shoving her into Ruth. They staggered on stage in front of a garishly painted set depicting magnolia trees in bloom and a yellow full moon in a Southern night sky. After a four-bar intro, the girls began their dance routine. Lily concentrated on keeping up with the steps and not tripping over her own feet. Then the number was over. The chorus line ran off the stage.

"I did it!" Lily picked Ruth up and twirled her around. The other girls rolled their eyes, but Lily didn't care.

"Nice job, baby." Lily whirled around to come face-to-face with Jobyna. She wore a calf-length sky-blue dress covered in fringe and hundreds of crystals that caught the bright stage lights, and a cloche hat with two white ostrich feathers. Before Lily could react, the announcer shouted over the crowd's roar that grew louder with each phrase.

"Ladies and gentlemen, the one you've all been waiting for, the Empress of Blues, the one and only Jobyna Jones." Jobyna bowed her head and waited as the crowd noise swelled until it seemed that a riot might break out. Then she walked on stage and strolled to the very front, just behind the footlights.

Lily peeked at the crowd from behind the heavy curtain. The audience was dressed in its Sunday best, men in stiff white collars and ties, and women in hats and gloves. They closed their eyes and smiled, swaying in their seats as a trumpet intro started "A Good Man is Hard to Find." Jobyna began to sing, and the audience clapped along in time with the music and her mellow voice.

Ruth, standing next to Lily, mimicked Jobyna's gestures and mouthed the words of the song, making Lily smile. "She's got them hypnotized," she whispered in Ruth's ear.

"She knows them. She's singing about their lives, too."

For an hour, Jobyna sang one soulful song after another, the crowd insisting on just one more. Finally, she signaled the band and they started "St. Louis Blues," and the audience rose with a roar to their feet.

Ruth whispered, "This is usually her last song. I bet they won't let her go, though."

After the number, the applause went on and on. Jobyna took bow after bow, recognized the musicians behind her, and finally when the audience wouldn't stop, she stepped up to the footlights again.

"Alright. We do have one more that we know. This is a special nod to my good friend Ma Rainey. It's about a cheating man. Any of you ladies know one of them?" Every woman in the audience roared, clapping and laughing and slapping their men on the shoulder. "'See See Rider,'" Jobyna announced and nodded to the piano player. Before the end of the raunchy song, everyone, women and men alike, was standing and clapping in time.

Jobyna took her final bows, and the gaggle of chorus girls watching from the wings parted to give her a clear path to exit the stage. Ruth handed her a towel to wipe the perspiration from her face. "Thank you, Ruthie." Jobyna headed toward her dressing room. "You and Lily come back to my room when the train gets started for Memphis."

Chapter Five

JOBYNA'S TENNESSEE TOE-TAPPERS Revue car, hooked up to the Louisville and Nashville Railroad train, left Nashville station at midnight and headed northwest across the Kentucky border to connect with a direct line south again to Memphis. Ruth said they would have to sit till dawn on a siding waiting for the southbound train.

Lily changed her position in the top bunk for what must have been the hundredth time. She squinted to read her book in the faint light from the lamp over her berth. The night before—her first in the sleeper car—she went right to sleep from a combination of exhaustion and the pleasantly soothing sway of the train car along the tracks.

Most of the girls complained bitterly about the cramped quarters and having to share the small lavatory, but Lily felt safe and sheltered in the narrow space. As for sharing the lavatory, it was a great improvement over her sister's house on the cotton farm outside Chattanooga, where the lavatory was a path from the kitchen door to an outhouse in the backyard.

Tonight, with the train stopped dead still on a siding, there was no rhythmic motion to rock her to sleep. She soothed herself by remembering every detail of the private midnight supper she and Ruth had shared with Jobyna in her parlor. Lily had never seen anything like the formal place settings of silver, china, and crystal. She hoped she was using the right fork or spoon as a waiter served each course.

She was too nervous to talk and was relieved that Ruth kept peppering Jobyna with questions about her music, her connection with the audience, and how she could sing those sad songs as though it had all actually happened to her. *Had the sad things she sang about all happened to Jobyna?*

"I can sing about those people's lives because I know the people in the audience. Every woman has some bitch trying to take away her man, so when I sing about it, I'm singing about what happened to her. It's not about me or my story, but about her."

"See, I told you, Lily. She knows them." Ruth turned back to Jobyna. "What about the men in the audience? They clap and yell as loud as the women."

"The man knows what he's done. He can't help how he is, but me singing the blues is a way for him to get told off about how he acts without a fight with his own woman. And he can think that he may have been bad, but he wasn't near as bad as my man was to me." Jobyna threw her head back and laughed. She looked over at Lily. "Get Jobyna another drink, baby."

Lily walked over to the bar with the empty glass. She took her time filling the drink from a crystal decanter. When Lily turned, Ruth was still chattering on, but Jobyna's total focus was on Lily's body. Her gaze moved from her survey of Lily's figure up to her eyes. Blood rushed to Lily's head.

Jobyna spoke to Ruth but kept her eyes locked with Lily's. "Ruthie, I'm invited to a rent party tomorrow night in Memphis after the show. You girls want to go?"

"Yes," Lily answered before Ruth could accept.

A snort from Ruth's bunk below interrupted Lily's musing about Jobyna and their dinner. Lily leaned over the side of the upper bunk and parted the velvet curtains on Ruth's bed. "Ruthie," Lily whispered. "Are you asleep?"

"Yes, and you should be, too."

"Ruth, what's a rent party?"

"Shhhh!" came a rude whisper from across the aisle.

Lily climbed down from her bed and crawled into Ruth's. Ruth turned to face the wall and punched her pillow. "Keep your cold feet off me," she mumbled.

"Ruth," Lily whispered in her ear. "What's a rent party?"

"Lily, you are too stupid to live. A rent party is when your rent is too high for you to afford that week. You have a party and pass the hat so you can pay your rent and not get thrown out on your dumb ass. That's a rent party, now leave me alone. Go to sleep."

***

Lily knew Ruth had danced with the show the year before at the Beale Street Palace Theater in Memphis. Lily pumped her with endless questions about what it would be like.

"Why do you need to know all this? You need to just be the best dancer you can. That will be enough for you to handle right now."

"Maybe knowing will make me a better dancer."

"Not likely. Well, it's the biggest theater in the South for colored only. The reason Jobyna and Little T like it so much is that every Thursday night after the regular show at eight o'clock they put on the Midnight Revel, and they let white people come but they have to sit in the balcony. Since Jobyna gets paid by the number of customers, Thursday at the Palace means a double payday for us."

"We get paid double, too?" Lily calculated how much more she'd be able to send back home to Martha.

Lily was standing backstage as Jobyna finished her last number of the midnight show and headed offstage to the sound of thunderous applause and stamping feet. The singer's face glistened with perspiration. This time Lily was ready with a towel for her.

Out of the corner of her eye, Lily could see Hattie standing with her arms crossed, frowning at her. Hattie turned and angrily clicked away in her tap shoes.

Ruth pulled Lily to the side. "Don't worry about Hattie," she said in Lily's ear. "But if you're trying to be close to Jobyna, here comes someone you do need to worry about."

Little T strutted over to Jobyna. He wore a suit that fit his small frame so well it must have been hand-tailored. His oxblood-and-white wingtips were spotlessly shined. He walked up to Jobyna, took her elbow, and spoke to her in a low voice.

Watching them, Lily suppressed a giggle. Jobyna was several inches taller than Little T and outweighed him, too. He reminded Lily of a yappy little dog that used to bother her sister's cow in Chattanooga. The lion's head on Little T's watch chain bounced back and forth as he gestured. Jobyna stood with her arms folded and nodded without saying a word. Little T turned and stormed off. Jobyna looked up at Lily with a smile. Lily felt a tingle in her stomach as Jobyna walked over to her.

"What was he so mad about?" Lily asked.

"He's just laying down the law about who he wants me to see and how he wants me to behave. He's got to drive the band bus to New Orleans tonight for our next gig, so he won't be here to watch after me in person."

"Why do you let him talk to you like that?" As soon as the words came out of Lily's mouth, she was afraid that she might have stepped over a line, but to her relief, Jobyna smiled as she shook her head.

"He's just looking out for me. The truth is, I can get a little carried away sometimes."

Maybe Jobyna was glad to have someone who cared about her, not as the star on the stage singing rough and raunchy blues, but as a person, even if he expressed his caring like a bully.

"So, we're not going to the rent party?" Lily felt a deep disappointment that she would not be with Jobyna on a new adventure—new for her, anyway.

"Sure we are, baby." Jobyna gently pushed a soft curl out of Lily's eye and behind her ear. "Go get dressed. Let's get out of here. Meet me outside the stage door in the alley."

Lily ran to find Ruth. They changed as quickly as they could in the packed dressing room. Lily crowded out three other girls to stand before the only full-length mirror in the room. Her dress was the same one she wore to her audition in Chattanooga, the only one she owned that she guessed would be presentable at a rent party. She was satisfied with her reflection in the mirror. The light floral fabric of the dress clung to her figure in all the right places. She touched up her lipstick and pulled on her cloth coat, urging Ruth out the door, down the hallway, and through the stage door that opened onto an alley alongside the theater off Beale Street. The women were in such a rush that they almost bumped into the bright yellow Duesenberg town car parked outside the door with the engine idling and a driver in a chauffer's cap behind the wheel.

Lily froze. "Is that for us?"

"I guess so. Don't ask so many questions."

Before they could decide whether or not to crawl into the car, the stage door opened and Jobyna walked out, followed closely by Hattie. Jobyna was wearing a red spangled dress with rows of sequins that glittered in the light from above the stage door. Tight curls peeked from under a matching red cloche hat. Hattie was wearing Jobyna's full-length mink. Lily tightened the belt of her cloth coat.

"Well, hop in, girls. Let's get there before all the fried chicken's gone." Jobyna sat up front with the driver, which put Lily in the back wedged between Hattie and Ruth.

The big car turned south on Main Street and glided through the night past apartment buildings, clothing stores, beauty salons, and diners. Ruth leaned over the back of the front seat. "Where is the party at, Jobyna? How long will it take us to get there?"

Jobyna reached across the seat and handed her a white card, the size that a businessman or a traveling salesman might pass out. Lily peeked over her shoulder and read the invitation aloud.

Not too slow and not too fast
But a real good time while it last

28

Come to
-: *A Party* :-
--- Given by ---
Ada and Rachel
301 Main Street, Apartment 3C

"Where did you find this?" Ruth asked.

"I didn't find anything. You have to be specially handed one, and they only go to the right people."

Hattie pulled a mason jar full of clear liquid from her beaded purse. "And if you ain't right yet, it's time to get right." She unscrewed the lid and passed it to Jobyna in the front seat, who took a big swig and passed the jar back. Hattie took a drink and offered it to Lily. Lily hesitated, and Hattie gave the jar a swirl. The fumes drifted up into Lily's face, burning her nose and making her eyes water. Hattie's smirk was a challenge.

Lily felt Jobyna watching her.

"Don't make her drink if she doesn't want to, Hattie."

Lily took the jar and drank from it, suppressing a cough, and then passed it to Ruth. By the time the Duesenberg stopped in front of an ordinary looking apartment building, they had killed almost the whole jar among the four of them.

Outside the car on the sidewalk, Lily stood looking up at the third floor where a pink light shone in an open front window. She wondered who the Ada and Rachel on the card might be. Sounds of a jazz piano and trumpet drifted over the empty, early morning Memphis street.

Hattie grabbed Jobyna's arm, and Lily and Ruth fell in behind as the four women climbed two flights of stairs to Apartment 3C. The front door was standing open. In the front room, which usually served as a bedroom, two beds were pushed up against the walls and the rug was rolled up to provide a makeshift dance floor, crowded with couples. The music Lily heard from the street came from a three-piece band playing in the corner.

Jobyna navigated the group through the gyrating dancers to a kitchen where a chrome and Formica table was covered with food: fried chicken, pork chops, pigs' feet, potato salad, and greens. A young woman, Ada or Rachel, rushed back and forth between the stove and the table, filling up bowls and platters and collecting payment from the long line of customers. There was another steady stream of people going into the bathroom emptyhanded and coming out with a mason jar full of liquor in each hand.

Two couples, loud and tipsy, butted in front of Lily in the food line. By the time she got her plate and picked up fried chicken, greens, and potato salad, she had lost sight of Jobyna and the others. She fumbled with her purse to pay Ada/Rachel, but the woman pointed in the general direction of the dance floor. "She already paid for you,"

Lily found a vacant space of wall to lean against and wolfed down the food as quickly as she could before looking around for where to put the empty plate. The liquor she drank in the car, the heat from all the bodies crammed into the small space, and the cigarette smoke that hung in a blue haze above the dancers' heads were combining to make Lily dizzy. She struggled to strip off her coat while balancing her plate.

"Here, pretty lady, let me help you with that." His voice, so close to her ear, made her jump. He was tall and thin, dressed in a windowpane-plaid suit and a fedora. Lily let him hold her coat while she shrugged out of it, then, lacking any place to put the coat, folded it over her arm. He took the empty plate from her hand and set it on the floor against the baseboard. "I'm Lester." He extended his hand.

"Lily."

"'And why take ye thought for raiment?'" His voice was soft as he leaned close to her and looked her up and down. "'Consider the lilies of the field, how they grow; they toil not, neither do they spin.'"

The quote from the Bible, out of context with her surroundings and combined with his tone, made Lily uneasy.

He chuckled. "Can I get you a drink, or maybe you like to smoke?" He held up a tightly rolled joint, lit it, and pushed it into Lily's face.

From nowhere, Jobyna was beside them. "Get away from her," she growled at Lester.

"Who are you, her mama?"

Neither woman responded.

"Unless you her mama, I think she can decide for herself." His smile showed a row of straight white teeth against his dark skin. He shoved the joint into Lily's face again. She reflexively drew back.

Jobyna grabbed his forearm. "If you push your hand toward her again, you'll draw back a bloody stump."

There was a tense moment of silence while Lester's eyes flicked back and forth between Lily and Jobyna, appearing to calculate his chances of overcoming the large and angry woman against the possibility that Lily would be interested in him. "Oh, I get it." He jerked his arm out of Jobyna's grasp. "She's your girlfriend. Well, you need to keep track of her better or she'll find out what a real one feels like."

Jobyna moved fast. She slammed her forearm into his chest, shoving him against the wall. His heel caught Lily's empty plate and his feet slipped out from under him, sending him crashing to the floor in a heap.

Jobyna leaned over to get in his face. "Shut your filthy mouth." She grabbed Lily's arm and headed her through the crowd, out the front door of the apartment, and down the stairs.

Lily stopped and looked back toward the apartment. "What about Ruth and Hattie?"

"They can take a cab."

Jobyna pushed Lily into the back seat of the big car. Before they could pull away from the curb, Ruth and Hattie came flying out of the apartment building and jumped in. Jobyna directed the driver to take them to Memphis Central Railroad Station.

Lily waited for her breathing to return to normal. "I hope we didn't ruin Ada and Rachel's rent party."

The three other women turned in unison to stare at her, and then Jobyna broke the silence with her huge laugh. "That's what you're worried about? Lily. Honey." She patted Lily's arm, and her touch left a tingle.

Chapter Six

LONG AFTER THE TRAIN pulled away from the Memphis station headed south for New Orleans, Lily lay awake in the pitch black of her windowless bunk. The velvet curtains, swaying in sync with the train, brushed her bare leg below her nightgown like the soft touch of a lover. Rather than soothing her as usual, tonight the motion of the train made her feel restless and unable to go to sleep.

She pictured how the stations must look as the *Panama Limited* churned its way down through the middle of Mississippi, stopping in towns along the way to take on or let off passengers. Finally, she climbed down from her berth, trying not to wake Ruth or the other sleeping girls, and carefully duck-walked along the narrow aisle toward the lavatory, balancing her body to stay in the middle and away from the lower bunks.

The curtain covering the etched glass window in the door leading to Jobyna's parlor was parted enough to show a slit of light. Lily couldn't resist the temptation to peek through. The parlor area was dark, but a bedside lamp shone on Jobyna sitting up in bed. She wore glasses and was writing in a notebook. As Lily watched, Jobyna laid her writing aside and came into the darkened parlor. Lily ducked away from the window then peeked again. Jobyna poured a glassful of liquor at the bar and took the drink back to her bed.

Lily inhaled a deep breath, held it, and knocked lightly. Jobyna didn't respond. Lily eased open the door and slipped through. The click of the latch got Jobyna's attention. Lily saw her squint into the darkness.

"Hattie?"

"No, Jobyna. It's me, Lily."

"What is it?"

Lily couldn't tell from her tone if she was annoyed or surprised. "I...I couldn't sleep, and I saw your light and I..." Lily stopped mid-sentence, unable to think of what she could possibly say next. To her relief, Jobyna patted the bed by her side.

"Crawl in here beside me. You're barefooted!"

Lily ran the last few steps and jumped in the bed under the covers. "What are you writing?"

"A song."

"What about?"

"About people who can't pay their rent because the landlord charges them three or four times what he should and so they have to live crowded into small rooms with too many other people."

"Like Ada and Rachel?"

Jobyna chuckled. "Yes, like Ada and Rachel."

Lily thought of Lester's insinuating whispers in her ear. The memory made her shiver.

"Cold?" Jobyna put her arm around Lily's shoulders and pulled her closer, then went back to writing.

"Jobyna."

"Mmm?" Lily was close enough to feel the slight rumble of the response in her chest.

"I know what that man meant when he said I'm your girlfriend."

Jobyna didn't answer right away. She took off her glasses and laid them on the bedside table with the pencil and notebook.

"You do?"

"He was saying that we are together like a man and woman would be."

"What do you know about that, Lily?"

"I've been with a man. Last summer. We did it twice. He wanted to very much, and I let him, but I didn't like it. He said it would be better the second time, so I did it again, but that was worse because I knew what to expect. After the second time, I hid when he came around. He finally stopped trying."

"You just haven't been with the right man yet, baby. Listen, that idiot at the rent party didn't know what he was talking about. Don't worry about his foolishness."

Lily wanted to tell Jobyna that she not only knew what the man was talking about, but that she wanted what he said to be true. She wanted to be Jobyna's girlfriend, and she dared to hope that the way Jobyna looked at her meant that she wanted Lily, too. But what about Hattie? And then there was Little T. What did he mean to Jobyna?

To Lily's disappointment, Jobyna said, "You better go back to your bed, Lily. We'll be in New Orleans when the sun comes up. We've got to be ready for two shows tonight and one every night for the next week. Little T found us a place to stay near the theater, so you girls will have real beds to sleep in for a week." She pulled back the covers. "Go on now."

Lily walked through the dark parlor. Again, she felt Jobyna's eyes following her with what she hoped was more than casual interest.

***

Lily imagined a modest, shabby rooming house similar to the building where they went to the rent party in Memphis. Jobyna and the chorus girls piled out of taxis that brought them from the train station to the rooming house on Basin Street in New Orleans where they would spend the week. Lily took in the four-story mansion with white columns across the marble front porch. "Ruth, this is a palace."

"No, it's not." Ruth sniffed. "This is a whorehouse, or at least used to be when whoring was legal in this neighborhood. The madam must have turned it into a boarding house. We're in Storyville, girl."

"What's Storyville?"

"Right here. Look around. This is where the good people of New Orleans decided they would let madams operate fancy houses as long as they stayed tucked away within the boundaries. Then the War came along, and the federal government thought whoring in plain sight might corrupt too many soldiers, so they shut Storyville down."

"How do you know all this, Ruthie, and why am I so ignorant?"

"I know because my mama told me about the real world. You've spent all your life with your nose in fairy-tale books." She grabbed Lily's hand. They followed Jobyna up the wide marble steps. "I sure hope they changed the mattresses before we got here."

Jobyna led the girls through the carved double doors into a foyer with a huge crystal chandelier, so big that it covered most of the ceiling. On the right was a parlor full of fancy dark furniture, upholstered with loud-colored fabric. Lily half expected to see women in French underwear draping their bodies around on the furniture, but there was only one person in the room. A slight man with caramel-colored skin sat behind an antique desk in the middle of the room. He rose and bowed formally. He wore a cutaway coat, striped pants, a pale grey silk ascot tie with a diamond stickpin, and white spats.

He rushed forward, grabbed Jobyna by both shoulders, pulled her toward him for an air-kiss beside each ear, and gushed, "Mademoiselle Jobyna. *Bienvenue a ma chere.* Welcome to New Orleans. Madam Ladeaux wanted to be here to greet you in person, but unfortunately the press of business has called her elsewhere. She adores you...your music that is. She will be in the front row for both your shows tonight.

And Saturday night after your closing show, with your permission, of course, we will be hosting a gala for the *gens d'élite,* the best people, in our fair city."

The man stopped for a breath. Jobyna gave Lily a sideways look with raised eyebrows.

"Oh, my goodness, please forgive my manners." He bowed deeply from the waist. "I am Anthony Chalamet, at your service for your entire stay. And for the rest of the ladies, of course." He turned, took a stack of heavy brass room keys from the desk, and passed them out among the girls. "Your room numbers are printed on the fobs. Mademoiselle Jobyna, you will be occupying the Governor's Suite on the fourth floor, with just the most divine view of the river." He picked up Jobyna's valise and led her to a tiny, two-person elevator in the foyer, chattering on the whole way in a mix of English and French.

Lily found her room number on the third floor. She pushed open the heavy door and looked around at the room. It was larger than her sister's whole house in Chattanooga. There was a mahogany bed with a thick down-filled mattress. She even had her own bathroom. She tested the water taps and found hot running water. *What must Jobyna's Governor's Suite look like?* While she unpacked her small bag, she daydreamed that Jobyna might invite her up to see the suite.

Audiences at the New Orleans Orpheum Theater were Standing Room Only for both shows. Their enthusiasm and adoration of Jobyna were as strong and loud as the shows in the other Southern cities they played. No matter how many times the Toe-Tappers danced, however, Lily got no better at the routine. Max, the show's director, felt the same way about her lack of dancing skills. After the first show at the Orpheum, he muttered in Lily's direction. "It's a good thing you look the way you do, girlie." And Little T seemed to save his nastiest scowls for her. What would happen if Max or Little T kicked her off the tour? Would Jobyna save her?

At two o'clock in the morning, after the second performance in the Orpheum, Ruth and Lily walked together arm-in-arm up Canal Street toward their fancy rooming house. The Canal Street cable car rumbled by, brightly lit against the dark, empty street. There were only two or three late-night dozing riders. Lily wondered if these people were going somewhere, or just using the cable car as a safe place to sleep.

Lily looked over at Ruth. "I'm afraid Max or Little T will fire me from the show."

"They can't fire you as long as Jobyna wants you. Plus, they never fire a girl in the middle of a tour unless she gets arrested or is too drunk or beat up to go on the stage. Why you talking like this, girl?"

"Max has given up on me getting any better. Little T looks at me like he wants to chew me up and spit me out. I still don't understand what Little T is to Jobyna."

"Little T's been with Jobyna since the beginning. He's her front."

"What do you mean, her front?"

"She needs a man out in front of her in this business. He hauls the band around between gigs and keeps them in line, as much as he can. He thinks he keeps Jobyna in line, too, but from what I can see she does what she wants to do. He argues with T-O-B-A and the theater owners when they try to cheat Jobyna on what's due her. And I heard he's talking to a recording company about Jobyna making phonograph records."

"Is he her man?"

"That's none of my business, or yours, either. I just notice that everybody is careful not to get between the two of them, even Hattie. All she does is talk big."

"Hattie said she can handle Jobyna. What did she mean?"

"That's none of your business, either. You need to concentrate on looking good up on that stage." Ruth jerked Lily closer. "Don't worry about how good you dance. You need to relax, that's all. You're too stiff. Saturday night at the party, we'll get some whiskey in you and practice on the dance floor."

Chapter Seven

AFTER THE SHOW ON Saturday night, the talk in the dressing room was about the party Madam Ledeaux was throwing for Jobyna back at their rooming house. All the best of New Orleans society was invited. Little T had come through the dressing room earlier to distribute the girls' pay and the mood was lively. The chorus girls elbowed each other for space in front of the mirror so they could take off their stage makeup and put on fresh for the party.

Lily hung back, fingering the fabric of her only presentable dress, the one that Jobyna had seen a million times. She watched Hattie and the rest of the girls pull on their silk stockings and wiggle into short flapper dresses spangled with crystal beads and covered with fringe and sparkling sequins.

"Hattie, your bosom is too big for that dress," one of the girls said. "You look like you're about to fall out of the top. Why don't we trade."

"Don't you worry about my bosom," Hattie shot back. "You take care of your own self."

Ruth talked Lily into splurging on a taxi back to the rooming house. "All you do is send your pay back to your sister in Chattanooga. She won't miss the twenty-five cents you spend on a taxi ride."

The Saturday night crowd of tourists ambling down the middle of Bourbon Street made the trip slow going. "We could have walked and got there faster," Lily said, still worrying about wasting money on the taxi. The car rattled down the uneven paving stones of the old street. Music spilled out from the open doors of each speakeasy they passed, the jazzy sounds from one overlapping and blending into the next.

They pulled up in front of the rooming house and got out of the car. Ruth opened her purse and waved Lily away. "Go on, girl. It's my treat. I'm tired of hearing you gripe." Lily kissed her on the cheek and ran up the front steps.

Inside, the formal parlor was a hive of activity. Footmen in cutaway coats, striped pants, and white gloves were setting up bars in each corner of the room and popping the corks from bottles of champagne. Young women in black maids' uniforms with starched white aprons and caps were loading two buffet tables with tureens of gumbo and heaping trays of crawdads, shrimp, and raw oysters on beds of ice. Anthony Chalamet bustled back and forth, snapping his fingers, fussing with the flower arrangements and generally ordering people around.

On a minstrels' balcony overlooking the room, a five-piece band tuned up, each musician playing his own random scales that added to the general noise level.

Lily ran up the stairs to her room, thinking she would try to do something new with her hair—anything to help herself feel more like she fit in with the fancy crowd that would soon be arriving. Sitting in the middle of her bed was a large white box, tied with a pink satin ribbon. She looked around the room waiting for whoever put the box there to suddenly jump out from behind the bathroom door and yell, "Surprise!"

She untied the ribbon and opened the box. Inside was the most beautiful dress she had ever seen. It was white lace, covered with crystals that sparkled like diamonds interwoven in the fabric. She held the dress up to the light. It gave the appearance of being see-through. There was an underlayer of material that exactly matched the color of her skin. In the box underneath the dress was a pair of white silk shoes and a headband covered with the same diamond-like crystals that highlighted a white ostrich feather. Lily pawed through the tissue paper, but there was no card. Could someone have made a mistake? Was the beautiful dress meant for someone else? She held the dress up to her in front of the wardrobe mirror. It seemed to be just her size. There was a knock on her door. She went to answer, still holding the dress.

Jobyna stood in the doorway, leaning against the jamb. She wore a silk dressing gown and held a champagne bottle and two crystal glasses. "Hold the dress up to you, baby." She looked Lily up and down. "Umm-hmm. I thought that would suit you."

"Jobyna, is this for me? It's beautiful. It's the most beautiful dress in the world."

Jobyna came into the room and sat on the bed. "You want to show all these fancy people how high class our show is, don't you? Your looks in that dress will be good advertising." She poured two glasses of champagne and handed one to Lily. "Drink this and then put on the dress. I deserve a preview, don't you think?"

Lily tipped the glass and drank the champagne in one gulp. She turned toward the bathroom door with the dress.

"I meant put it on out here, baby." Jobyna leaned back on the bed, propping herself on her elbows and smiling a crooked smile.

Lily unbuttoned her cotton dress, dropped it in a puddle around her feet, and stepped out of it. She was relieved that she was wearing her best slip. As Jobyna's eyes traveled up and down her figure, Lily felt her nipples harden against the fabric of her slip. She stepped into the white lace dress and began to pull it up over her hips. There was a loud banging on her door.

Little T's voice rang out. "Jobyna." Bang, bang, bang. "I know you're in there. Open the door."

Lily stepped out of the dress and held it up in front of her.

Jobyna put her finger to her lips and shook her head.

Bang, bang, bang. "Open this door." Little T's voice rose to a higher pitch.

Lily went to the door and looked through the peephole. "It's Lily. I'm not dressed, Little T." She held her breath and waited. "I'm not dressed."

"Jobyna's in there." To Lily's relief, his voice sounded a little more tentative.

Lily looked over at Jobyna, who shook her head again. "No, she's not. I'm getting dressed for the party. What do you want?" Lily struggled to keep her voice steady. There was a moment of silence, then she heard him muttering and the taps on his shoes clicking as he strode away down the marble hallway. She pictured his retreating back and wondered if he had the gun stuck in his waistband. She turned to Jobyna, still sitting on the bed.

"Shouldn't you go? What if he comes back with a key?"

"Don't worry about Little T. I'll take care of him." Jobyna rose from the bed. "Put on your pretty dress." She crossed the room and took Lily by both shoulders. She pulled Lily's face to hers and placed a gentle kiss on her lips. "I'll see you down at the party." She opened the door, peered up and down the hallway, and left.

Lily leaned against the closed door, trying to get her balance, disoriented by the unexpected kiss. She brushed her fingers across her lips, trying to figure out what the kiss meant.

***

Lily hesitated on the stair landing above the crowd of merrymakers. A hardwood dance floor, laid down in the large parlor for the party, was packed with couples doing the latest dance steps in rhythm with music from the jazz band. Lily looked for Jobyna, but no luck. She scanned the room again, looking to locate someone she knew. She spotted Ruth holding a champagne glass and talking to a tall, distinguished-looking middle-aged white man in a tuxedo.

Lily took a deep breath, smoothed her dress over her thighs, and descended the steps. At the bottom, a waiter presented a silver tray loaded with glasses of champagne. She took one and began weaving her way through the crowd, holding her full glass over her head to avoid spilling on herself or someone else. She headed toward Ruth and the man, but then saw him bend over and whisper in Ruth's ear. She stopped short, hesitating to interrupt what looked like an intimate moment.

The band finished a ragtime tune and played a loud fanfare. The crowd turned its attention to a small stage in the front of the room. From behind a screen sprang a stout figure dressed in white tie and tails, a black silk top hat, and shiny patent leather shoes. He bounced his cane on the floor, spun around, and caught it neatly on the rebound. The crowd went wild, clapping and laughing. The band struck up the intro to an upbeat dirty blues song made famous by Ma Rainey, "Prove It on Me Blues."

The performer began to sing. Lily's mouth fell open. It was Jobyna singing the suggestive lyrics about a woman who preferred the romantic company of other women. The crowd roared. Jobyna caught Lily's eye and winked at her. Lily shook her head and clapped along with the rest.

Jobyna strutted back and forth across the tiny stage. After several verses the song ended to whistles and loud applause. A woman in a red dress ran forward and pulled Jobyna onto the dance floor. Other women lined up to cut in for their turn to dance with her.

Lily stood on the sidelines, sipping her champagne and watching the dancers. Ruth came up behind her and pinched her waist. "Look at you, girl. That dress is something."

"Jobyna got it for me. She said I'd be good advertising for the show." Lily twirled around to show off the dress.

"What did I tell you about your looks being your ticket." Ruth grabbed two full glasses of champagne from a passing waiter's tray.

"Who was that man you were talking to?" Lily asked.

"That is the mayor of New Orleans."

"Where did he go?"

"He's 'circulating,' but he'll be back. "

"Ruthie, is he married?"

Ruth drained her champagne. "He may be but remember what the song says: whatever you do, they've got to prove it on you."

Chapter Eight

LILY WALKED OUT THE open French doors onto the terrace of Madam Ladeaux's rooming house and breathed deeply of the sweet-smelling, velvety New Orleans night air. She crossed the flagstones and stuck her nose near the honeysuckle vine that grew along the back fence of the small courtyard.

"This is a relief from the crowd, yes?"

Lily jumped, startled by the unexpected male voice an arm's length behind her. She turned to see a tall young man, formally dressed, with wavy blond hair and a pencil-thin light mustache. She could hear a slight accent, maybe German.

"I didn't mean to interrupt." He backed up a step.

Lily shook her head. "I'm just enjoying the honeysuckle."

He walked to the flower-covered vine and pulled a blossom. "Did you know that you can taste the nectar just as the hummingbird does?" He stepped closer to Lily, pinched the end off the flower, and placed it in Lily's hand. "A wonderful English word, yes? Honeysuckle. Suck the juice."

A small bubble of juice glistened on the end of the blossom. She touched her tongue to the flower. "It tastes like it smells."

"Just so. I'm Leo Bruno. Would I be forward to tell you that I've been watching you all evening? Are you from the city, or are you with the show?"

"I'm one of Jobyna's dancers."

"You're a professional dancer yet you haven't been dancing tonight." Leo leaned against the trunk of a tree, his hands in his pockets. He seemed perfectly relaxed.

"I'm not a very good dancer." Lily looked toward the open door, wishing she was back with the crowd.

Leo raised his eyebrows and laughed. "A professional dancer who can't dance?" He picked another honeysuckle blossom and sniffed it. "Do you know New Orleans well?"

"I've never been here before."

"Oh, you must let me take you to the Café du Monde tomorrow morning for café au lait and beignets. You've never tasted anything

better. Beignets are French-style donuts covered with powdered sugar."
He held up the blossom. "Sweeter than honeysuckle."

Lily shook her head. "I don't think so."

"I hope I haven't come on too strongly. If it seems so, it's only that I
don't understand your customs so well. Please tell me more about
yourself. Tell me about being in Miss Jobyna's show. She's quite a
character. What do you say in English...a bull dyke? She hates men, no?"

Lily felt heat flushing through her body. "You don't know anything
about her." Lily glanced again toward the open door and saw Jobyna
framed in the doorway. She turned and disappeared back into the
room.

"Goodbye, Mr. Bruno." She brushed past him and ran the few steps
to the door. She watched Jobyna grab Hattie by the hand, cross the
room, and push the button to summon the tiny elevator. Lily
suppressed the urge to call to Jobyna. She probably wouldn't be heard
anyway over the music and noise of the crowd.

Lily looked down at her beautiful dress and white silk shoes. The
crystals sparkled and winked under the lights of the chandeliers. How
would this evening be different if Little T hadn't banged on her door
earlier? Would Jobyna have held her in her arms, and could Lily have
found the words to tell her that she wanted to be with her like the man
said at the rent party? Between Little T's threatening presence and
Hattie's constant availability, Lily wondered if she would ever be able to
tell Jobyna how she felt about her. After New Orleans, there was only
one more tour stop in Mobile, Alabama. Lily wasn't sure what would
happen after the tour. She was afraid she might never see Jobyna again.

When Lily imagined putting her yearning into words to Jobyna, she
came up blank. Could she confide in Ruth? Her cousin was so much
more worldly and bold. Maybe she could help Lily find the words and
make a plan. Lily shook her head. *A plan for what?*

Ruth was in the middle of the dance floor, doing a vigorous
Charleston with not one but two handsome young male partners. She
caught Lily's eye and motioned her to join them, but Lily frowned and
shook her head.

The band finished the upbeat tune and announced a short break.
Ruth strutted over to Lily, fanning her flushed face with her hands.

"Where's the mayor?" Lily asked.

"Oh, he's more interested in poker than he is in me. He's in some
game they have going in a back room." She poked Lily in the ribs. "You
are such a stick-in-the-mud. What's wrong with you? You look like

you're at a funeral instead of the best party ever." Ruth turned her back to the dance floor and pulled up the hem of her dress to reveal a silver flask attached to her thigh by a red garter. She offered the flask to Lily. "Here, lighten up."

Lily took the flask and tipped it up for a deep swig, then tilted it for another.

"There you go. That's the spirit," Ruth said.

"Do you think Jobyna likes me, Ruth?"

"Of course."

"I don't mean just...like."

Ruth held her hand up. "You don't have to go on. I know what you mean. It's not my thing, but whatever. Of course, Jobyna likes you. Why do you suppose she gave you this dress?" Ruth fingered the lace material. "Do you think she really did it to advertise the show? This dress wasn't cheap, you know."

Lily couldn't stop the smile that spread over her features.

Ruth shook her head. "I thought you could tell she likes you. You have to let her know you're interested. Otherwise, she might think you're not. You just have to hope you're not too young and silly for her to mess with."

"I want her to mess with me."

"So, tell her." Ruth tucked the flask back into her garter. The band began to play again, and one of Ruth's dance partners ran over, grabbed her by the waist, and spun her onto the dance floor.

***

Lily stood in front of the tiny mirror over the washbasin in the cramped train lavatory that all the dancers shared. She ran cold water over her hands and scrubbed her face. She examined her bloodshot eyes with dark circles underneath, put there by lack of sleep.

The troupe had left the boardinghouse in New Orleans before dawn to board the train for their last tour stop in Mobile, Alabama. As they loaded their luggage into taxis to leave for the train station, the party was still going strong.

Brushing her teeth made Lily feel a little more human. She pulled the door open and peered back down the narrow aisleway between the berths. The curtains covering the dancers' beds swayed with the train's motion, but no one stirred. She turned and walked to her right, through the lounge area and past the kitchen. She paused at the door to

Jobyna's parlor. The light was on.

Lily took a deep breath, raised her hand, and knocked softly. She was almost relieved that there was no response. She turned to go, but then she heard the unmistakable clink of ice cubes in a crystal glass. She knocked again, more loudly.

"Come in." Jobyna sounded wide awake.

Lily pushed the door open. Jobyna was reclining on the chaise lounge with a book in one hand and a drink in the other. She put down the book and set her glass on top of it. "What is it, Lily?"

"I want to thank you for my dress, and I..." She hesitated. To her horror, her voice caught in a sob.

Jobyna took off her glasses and opened her arms. "Come to me, baby."

Lily knelt by the chaise and leaned into Jobyna's embrace. "Do you think I'm too young and silly to mess with?"

"Who put that in your head? Was it Ruth?"

Lily nodded.

Jobyna pulled Lily into her lap, smoothed her hair away from her forehead, and pressed her lips there. She whispered against Lily's skin. "Tell me what you want, Lily. You have to tell me."

"I want to be with you. I want to be special to you."

Jobyna nodded. She turned off the reading lamp and led Lily into the bedroom.

Chapter Nine

WHEN LILY WOKE, IT was daylight outside, the train was stopped, and she was alone under the mink coverlet. She took a minute to understand where she was, and then felt around under the covers for her nightgown. She picked up Jobyna's pillow and smelled the scent of rosewater that her hair had left behind.

Being with Jobyna was different from anything Lily had ever experienced or even dreamed of. It was like being enveloped by a strong but soft force. They fit together like a key in a lock, or two pieces of a puzzle. Jobyna was clearly experienced from being with many other women, but she was careful to go slowly with Lily. "You tell me if you want to stop, baby," she said, but Lily didn't want to stop. She was surprised at how natural it all felt to her. There were even times when she took the lead, giving Jobyna pleasure the same as the more experienced woman gave her.

Lily hugged the pillow to her chest. She heard a light knock at the door across the parlor. She dropped the pillow and held the covers up to her neck. "Who is it? Jobyna?" Silence. "Jobyna, is it you?" Still no answer. "Ruth?" She heard footsteps walking away from the door. She hurriedly pulled her gown on over her head and parted the curtain at the side window. The railroad car was parked by itself on a siding at a station. The sign above a double door read "Mobile." Red-capped porters were moving back and forth between the train car and the station, pushing carts loaded with suitcases, trunks, and racks of costumes.

There was another knock at the door, this time definite and loud. Ruth's voice rang out, "Lily, wake up." Lily ran barefoot to the door and flung it open.

"You've got to get dressed, girl." Ruth shoved Lily's cardboard valise through the door into her chest. "Everybody's left already. Jobyna sent me back to get you."

"Were you at the door earlier?"

"No. What are you talking about?"

"Someone knocked on the door. Do you think it was Hattie or Little T?"

"I don't know, but we don't have time for that now. If you're going to get all up in this situation, you're going to have to learn how to handle Hattie and Little T, too." Ruth grabbed the valise out of Lily's arms and opened it on the bed, pulling out the dress on top and digging around for a pair of shoes. "These will do for now. Jobyna says we have to go straight to the theater. Leave your suitcase here. We're not going to stay in Mobile tonight after the show. Little T says he can't find us a fitting place to stay in this cracker town. The people want to hear Jobyna sing the blues, but they don't want us in their fancy hotels."

The taxi let them off in front of the Saenger Theater. The three-story buff-colored brick building occupied a whole city block in downtown Mobile. On an ornate metal awning over the front entrance, Lily saw a crest with a sea dragon in the shape of the letter "S." Underneath it in fancy script was, "The Most Beautiful Playhouse in All of Dixie." Lily started toward the front entrance.

Ruth put a hand on her arm. "I don't think we go in that way. This is a white theater. Our entrance is this way." They walked around the corner of the building to a modest awning that said, "Colored Entrance. Admission 10 Cents." Inside, the backstage facilities were fancier than other theaters where the show played, with three floors of dressing rooms so that each chorus girl had only one roommate.

Max, Jobyna's show director, walked along the line of the dressing rooms, knocking on doors and calling for a rehearsal in fifteen minutes. "That last performance in New Orleans was too loose. You girls are getting lazy. We need to show these white folks that we are professionals."

Lily and Ruth rushed to pull on their rehearsal leotards and tap shoes. They descended the stairs to the stage behind the line of chorus girls. Lily lagged at the rear, hoping to avoid Hattie. Ruth said that she needed to learn how to deal with Hattie and Little T, but she wasn't anxious to start anytime soon.

While Max and the rehearsal piano player were consulting about the score, Lily and Ruth walked to the edge of the stage and looked out over the auditorium. The decorations reflected Mobile's Gulf Coast location. Mermaids swam in circles around three large chandeliers, and the ceiling was covered with figures of seahorses, shells, and fish molded in the plaster. Heavy draperies lined the walls. The aisles were covered with carpets with the name of the theater woven into the fabric.

"This is beautiful. Like something in a fairy-tale," Lily said.

"I know. The girls were saying that it's brand new, not even open officially yet. That's the only reason they're letting us play here. Once it opens, no more colored shows."

Rehearsal went on all afternoon. Max put them through the steps over and over, critiquing each girl harshly. Max was particularly critical of her. She hoped Ruth was right, that Jobyna wouldn't let Max fire her before their last performance.

As her mind was drifting back to her time with Jobyna the night before, the singer's voice rang out from the wings. "That's enough, Max. You're going to wear them out before the show even gets started." Lily could see Little T standing behind Jobyna glowering with his thumbs tucked in the vest of his three-piece suit. Lily didn't think it was her imagination that Little T gave her an even meaner look than usual. Did he know that she spent last night with Jobyna? Was he the one who knocked on Jobyna's door this morning?

Max clapped his hands and repeated his usual orders about being back on time for the show and to not bring any men around in the meantime. The chorus girls shuffled off toward their dressing rooms. Lily stopped and bent over, pretending to lace her tap shoes tighter, hoping to stall until she could talk to Jobyna. She watched Little T walk over to Max and start a conversation. He pointed toward the stage lights, giving Max instructions on how to light Jobyna during the show. He seemed to want to be the one who knew everything about what was best for the singer, both technical and business-wise as well as in her private life.

Jobyna made a subtle motion with her head that summoned Lily to follow her backstage. Jobyna led her behind the canvas scene of a harvest moon shining on an antebellum plantation house. She pulled Lily into her arms and kissed her deeply. "Are you feeling okay, baby?"

Lily's didn't trust herself to speak. She nodded.

"We're staying on the train tonight. Will you come to me?"

Lily nodded again.

"This is our last night on the road. The train leaves for Chattanooga before dawn."

"I know. What happens then?"

"We need to talk when we have some time." They heard the taps on the heels of Little T's shoes as he left the stage and climbed the stairs

49

headed toward Jobyna's dressing room. "I have to go. Come tonight, whatever time everyone settles down. They'll be celebrating late, I'm sure." She kissed Lily quickly and disappeared around the corner of the scenery.

Chapter Ten

JOBYNA'S PARLOR IN THE train car was jammed with people. The door to the bedroom had been opened to accommodate all the revelers. The crowd, celebrating the end of a successful tour, included all the cast and crew who traveled with the show plus Little T, Charlie Reed from the booking association, and Max, the show director. There were also several flashy young men busy flirting with the chorus girls. Lily thought these must be the stage-door Johnnys that Max warned the girls against at every rehearsal. The noise level rose as laughter and conversations competed with jazz music coming from a phonograph in the corner.

Lily edged her way through the crowd to the bar, covered with silver trays of fancy canapes and bottles of liquor. She poured amber liquid into a glass and drank half of it in one gulp. The bite of the liquor on her throat reminded her of her first taste of Jobyna's liquor and the coughing fit it caused. That seemed to have happened to a different girl in a different life.

She leaned against the bar, scanning the crowd for Jobyna and found her in the bedroom sitting on the bed talking to Hattie. The chorus girl suddenly stood up, spun around, and began to push her way through the crowd toward Lily.

Lily braced herself for a confrontation. She made a split-second decision that if a showdown was coming, she'd meet it head-on. As Ruth said, if she was going to be with Jobyna, she'd have to learn to deal with Hattie and Little T. She put her drink down on the bar and stood up tall. Hattie shoved past her without stopping and stormed out the door. Jobyna caught Lily's eye, smiled, and shook her head. She started across the room toward Lily.

Over the noise of the party, someone began tapping a crystal glass to draw the attention of the crowd. Charlie Reed dramatically cleared his throat. "Ladies and gentlemen, let me propose a toast." He raised his glass. "To the one and only, the toast of the Southland from Chattanooga to New Orleans to Mobile, the Empress of the Blues, Jobyna Jones."

Everyone held up their glasses and shouted, "Jobyna," and drank.

Little T encircled Jobyna's waist and pulled her to him. "Jobyna and

I want to thank you all for the success of our tour." He reached into his inside coat pocket and pulled out a stack of envelopes. "I have here your final pay, plus a surprise. Jobyna and I want to do more than give you lip service. These envelopes include a generous bonus for your hard work." He began handing out the envelopes to the delight of the band, dancers, and crew.

"And I have an announcement to make," Little T went on. "As soon as Jobyna gets the train car back home to Chattanooga tomorrow night, we're taking the band and leaving for Atlanta. There's an up-and-coming radio station there, owned by a rich white man. He saw our show and offered us a deal we can't refuse. I have negotiated an agreement for Jobyna to sing her music on the radio so that people all over the South can hear her."

A buzzing in Lily's head blocked out the enthusiastic applause of the crowd. She searched Jobyna's face for a clue of what Little T's announcement might mean to her hopes of being with the singer. Jobyna smiled and shook hands with the well-wishers, but she seemed to Lily, to be avoiding looking in her direction.

Lily left her glass on the bar and found her way to the door as tears gathered in her eyes. She stepped down onto the station platform, followed it past the squares of lights from the windows of the station, and stopped in the dark at the edge of the platform. She heard footsteps coming up behind her and felt Jobyna's strong arms wrap around her shoulders.

Jobyna turned Lily around to face her. Lily could smell the rosewater scent that for the rest of her life would remind Lily of this moment. "Listen to me, baby." Jobyna brushed the tears away from her cheeks. "I didn't know Little T was going to announce about the radio tonight. I was going to tell you first."

Lily turned her face away. "Were you going to tell me that you want me to go with you?"

Jobyna hesitated.

"You weren't, were you? I can't go with you because of Little T, right?"

"I just don't know what to expect. I don't know how much free time I'll have, or when you and I would be able to be together."

"Where will you be staying?"

"The radio station is on the top floor of the Biltmore Hotel in downtown Atlanta, but we'll probably need to get a room somewhere. I doubt they'll let us stay in the hotel. That's just one thing that I can't predict right now."

Lily shrugged out of Jobyna's hands and took a few steps away from her.

"Lily, give me a little time. Go back to your sister's in Chattanooga for a while. It'll be a few weeks at the most. Then I'll send for you." Jobyna looked toward the train car. "I have to go. Come back to the party with me. Did you get your pay?" She took Lily's elbow.

"Do you promise to send for me?"

"I promise." Jobyna leaned over and kissed her quickly. "Smile for me. That's my baby."

They walked to the railroad car. Jobyna went in first. Lily hung back, watching through the window as people hugged the singer and slapped Little T on the back. In the corner of the parlor, Ruth was talking and laughing with Charlie Reed. Lily grabbed the handrail and climbed the three steps into the car.

Ruth saw her come in and ran over to her. "Lily, I've been talking with Charlie Reed." She sounded giddy with excitement. "He says he can get us a spot in another tour. And the most exciting thing, he says he can get me on the bill as a singer, backup of course, but that's a start. He says that when people hear we've toured with Jobyna, it will be easy to get us on. I didn't sing with Jobyna, but they don't have to know that. We can go back to New Orleans from here. He'll meet us there." Ruth pulled the envelope with her pay out of her sleeve. "Look at this. With this money we can get a room in New Orleans, maybe even an apartment."

Lily shook her head. "I don't want to go with another tour. I'm going back to Chattanooga. I'm no singer. I'm not even good enough to dance in the chorus line."

"This is about Jobyna, isn't it?"

Lily was tempted to confide in Ruth, but instead she said, "I don't want to go on another tour. Plus, I don't trust Charlie Reed. And neither should you."

"Well, suit yourself, but I'm going to New Orleans. Reed promised he will use his connections for me." She grabbed Lily's shoulders and shook her. "Lily, I might get to sing!"

Lily hoped for Ruth's sake that she could trust Reed's promise. For herself, she hoped she could trust Jobyna's promise.

Chapter Eleven

HER SISTER MARTHA'S SMALL frame house in the country outside Chattanooga sat on the edge of the field, barely a few feet separating the rows of cotton plants from the whitewashed siding. Only rich people could afford the luxury of using good crop land as a yard. The narrow area between the front porch and a two-lane gravel road was covered with packed red clay.

Every afternoon at the same time, Lily brought a broom outside to sweep it. She wanted to be close to the mailbox when the mailman's Model T came by. He always stopped on the side of the road in front of the house, stepped out on the running board, and deposited her brother-in-law's *Chattanooga Times*. But so far, no letter from Jobyna with a bus ticket to Atlanta had arrived.

Lily leaned on the broom and shaded her eyes to peer up the road. The mail was later than usual today. She could hear Martha in the kitchen starting the cornbread for supper. Lily would have to put away the broom soon and help with the meal. She took a few more swipes then climbed the wooden steps, crossed the front porch, and pulled the screen door open.

The house was called a "shotgun." It was only one room wide—the living room, kitchen, and two bedrooms stacked one behind the other. The joke was you could shoot a shotgun from the front porch and out the back door without hitting anything. Lily watched Martha scurrying back and forth between the sink and the stove. Martha looked up without stopping. "No mail yet?"

Lily shook her head.

"Sometimes he's late," Martha said. Her older sister was a woman of few words, as though talking would take up too much time and effort. Lily was relieved that she hadn't asked any questions in the two weeks since she showed up at the front door with the borrowed cardboard suitcase.

Lily heard the crunching of the mailman's Model T's tires out front. She ran out the door to the road.

"Evenin'." He tipped his fedora and handed the mail to Lily, a newspaper tied up with twine, and a letter addressed to Lily. There was a postmark from Atlanta, but no return address. She stuffed the letter, unopened, into the pocket of her dress and went back into the kitchen.

Lily's brother-in-law, Carl, and their twin teenaged sons came in from the field and stopped on the back porch to wash their faces and hands. Lily and Martha served their supper at the kitchen table. As she bustled between the stove and the table, Lily heard the rustle of the letter in her pocket.

Carl pushed his chair away from the table and took his usual place in the living room with the newspaper. The women sat down to eat their supper. This was the time of day when the two sisters could sit together and when Martha relaxed enough to talk. Tonight, Lily was too anxious to linger over food. She wanted to find a private place to read her letter. She wolfed down a piece of cornbread and drank a glass of buttermilk, then began clearing the dishes.

Martha watched Lily start dishwater. "Is that all you're going to eat?"

"Not very hungry."

After she finished the dishes, she took a kitchen chair out to the front porch and positioned it in front of a window that reflected the light from Carl's reading lamp inside. She tore the letter open, took out two folded pages, and turned the envelope upside down and shook it. No bus ticket.

Dearest Lily,

By now I guess you've settled in at your sister's house. Things are taking a lot longer here than I thought they would. We came here with Little T's idea that we had a deal agreed to. The men who own the station seem to think different. They wanted to start over talking about the money once they saw we were anxious.

WSB calls itself "The Voice of the South" and it most certainly is the biggest station in Georgia, which means lots of white men in suits who think they're in charge. It seems to take a long time to make a decision, and I haven't even been on the radio yet. They have something called "sponsors," and that's a whole other group of men in suits who get a say-so about the music I'm going to sing. Little T spends all day sitting in their offices listening to them go on. They're paying us some to keep us talking, what they call an "option," so that's good, I guess. Thank the Lord it's Little T and not me that has to haggle with them.

I spend the days thinking about you and wishing things would get settled so I can send for you. I'm reading the newspaper for houses to rent so we can have someplace nice to live when you come. At night, Little T and the band and I go to clubs and I sing for free. I think I would go crazy otherwise.

Little T says that I should be actually singing on the radio in a week or two. I don't know whether he's just telling me what I want to hear or if he's really right about that. Between just you and me, he is learning all this as we go along. I asked him if we should get us a lawyer, but that sent him into a rant about all the sacrifices he's making for me and how good radio is going to be for my career and how we wouldn't be here without him. Sometimes I wish we had just rested a little then gone out for another tour, maybe up North this time.

Lily put the letter down in her lap. She thought about the sad look in Jobyna's eyes the first time she met her in the Chattanooga apartment, and then the happiness she saw in the railroad car as they were starting the tour. She picked up the letter again.

As soon as I start singing on the radio, I'll get us a house and send you a bus ticket. If Little T's right, that should be in two weeks. Do you want a house in town, or would you rather be out in the country? Atlanta is a big city; some people call it "The New York of the South." I'm not sure if they mean that as a good thing. It's not like anything you're used to. You might like that, though. Please write back to me right away in care of General Delivery. I'll pick it up at the post office. I want to know that you're alright and that you haven't lost faith in me.

The sound of the screen door interrupted her reading. Martha stuck her head out. "What are you doing out here? The mosquitos are liable to carry you off." They listened for a while to katydids chirping in the dark. "They're singing to call in the cold weather. Hard to believe as hot as it is right now, but we'll have frost in a few weeks." She stepped onto the porch, closed the screen door, and leaned against it. "Is that the letter you've been waiting for?"

Lily nodded.

"Carl and the boys have gone to bed. I'm fixin' to get ready to."

"You go ahead. I'll be in soon." Lily waited for the screen door to close and went back to reading the letter.

Please write to me soon. I'll check at the post office every day. All I do is walk around the city anyway or write songs. They're all about how

much I miss you.
    Yours until we're together,
    Jobyna

Lily carefully refolded the letter and put it back in its envelope. She pictured Little T in his fancy suit and handmade shoes. The lion's head watch fob dangling on his chest. She wondered if these white men who owned the radio station respected him or whether they made fun of him behind his back like Hattie and the other chorus girls. She sat motionless, listening to the katydids. Two more weeks. She blew out a sigh, pushed up from the chair, and went inside.

Chapter Twelve

WHEN JOBYNA'S FIRST LETTER came, Lily answered it the next day. She carefully placed her letter in the mailbox, raised the red metal flag that signaled outgoing mail, and watched from behind the screen door as the mailman's Model T pulled alongside the mailbox. He dropped off Carl's newspaper and picked up the letter.

Three weeks later, Lily and Martha sat on the porch swing trying to stay cool in the heat of midday southern Tennessee in the summer. Martha gently rocked them as she shelled black-eyed peas for supper. Lily closed her eyes and let the hypnotic rhythm of the swing soothe her mind.

Jobyna's letter said she expected to be singing on the radio by now, but Lily hadn't gotten another letter or a bus ticket to Atlanta. Lily's moods swung from disappointment to despair to hopefulness. Jobyna was in an unfamiliar situation that she wasn't in control of. She was doing the best she could. Hadn't she said she was looking for a house for them? That meant that she intended to keep her promise to send for Lily. But if she missed her as much as she said, she should just let Lily come to Atlanta. They would work it out together. Then Lily thought about the scowl on Little T's face every time he looked at her. Where would he be when she and Jobyna had their house? Not living there, too, surely.

The swing was a new addition to Martha's front porch. Carl and the boys rescued it from the caved-in porch of an abandoned sharecropper's house on the back edge of their forty-acre cotton farm. The three worked together in the barn one Sunday after church, scraping, sanding, and painting it bright green as a surprise for Martha.

Lily reached into Martha's bowl, took a handful of peas, and began to shell them into her lap. "It was really sweet of Carl to fix the swing for you. He loves you very much."

Martha smiled and nodded.

"Martha, how long does it take for a letter to get from Atlanta to here?"

"I don't know. Probably two or three days."

"Do letters ever get lost?"

"I guess it's possible, but I never heard of it." Martha set her bowl of peas aside and wiped her hands on her apron. "Are you going to tell me what's going on with you? It's about that singer, isn't it? You know you can stay here with us as long as you need to, but you're driving me to distraction with your moping around the place. I'm too busy for any nonsense."

"Does Carl want me to leave?"

"No, of course not. Carl is too soft-hearted to say a word. I'm not saying anybody wants you to leave, but we don't even have a room for you. It's not right for a young woman your age to be sleeping on the couch in the living room."

Lily thought about the money from her bonus at the end of the tour. It was hidden inside the lining of her winter coat. "I can pay you more. I try be useful."

"A little more money would help." Martha went back to shelling the peas. "I just hate to see you so unsettled. What is this woman to you anyway?"

"She's going to send for me. I'm going to Atlanta."

"To be in another show?"

Lily shook her head. How could she put together the words that would explain to her older sister that she wanted to be with Jobyna forever, not having to worry about the Hatties or the Little Ts? She would take care of Jobyna so that all she had to think about was singing for the audiences that loved her. Jobyna wouldn't need Little T at all. And Jobyna would make Lily feel safe and treasured all the rest of their lives.

"Jobyna isn't doing another show right now. She's going to be on the radio, as soon as they can get a deal straightened out. She's very good at the business side of entertainment."

"What's taking her so long, then?"

"Someone's handling it for her who maybe isn't so good at it."

Martha pushed herself off the swing, picked up her bowl of peas, and opened the screen door. "Well, I don't know anything about the business side of show business, but if she really wants to have you with her in Atlanta and you want to go there, seems to me you'd be there." She caught the screen door with her hip to keep it from slamming shut.

Lily thought again about the money hidden in her coat. She could buy a bus ticket to Atlanta for herself. But how would she find Jobyna?

She could go to the radio station. Jobyna had mentioned it was on the top floor of the Biltmore Hotel, but Jobyna might not have started there yet.

Lily heard pots and pans rattling in the kitchen. The noise was louder than it needed to be and was meant as a signal to her to come in and help Martha with the meal. She sighed and rose from the swing. As she headed through the front door, a vehicle approached on the gravel road that ran in front of the house. She heard the noise of tires crunching on the gravel and the pings of rocks jumping up to hit the undercarriage. She had come to recognize the sounds of the occasional pickup truck or tractor that passed, but this was different.

She turned toward the road and saw a long, yellow Duesenberg. It slowed and turned into the yard. The car had barely stopped before the back door swung open. Jobyna stepped out and spread her arms wide.

Lily burst through the screen door, jumped off the front porch, ignoring the steps, and threw herself into Jobyna's embrace. "You came for me!"

As usual, Jobyna was done up fit to kill. Her yellow silk dress and cloche hat were an exact color match with the long car that sat in front of the house with the engine ticking as it cooled down after the trip from Atlanta to Chattanooga.

Jobyna whirled Lily around and set her down, holding her at arm's length. "Baby, look at you. You're filling out. Must be all this good home cooking." She smiled at Martha, who had followed Lily out the door and was standing on the porch holding a black cast-iron skillet. "Just a minute," Jobyna said to Lily. She ducked back inside the car and came out with a package wrapped in colorful paper and tied with a pink satin ribbon.

Jobyna took Lily's hand and climbed the porch steps. "This must be the sister you've told me so much about. Martha, right? I'm Jobyna Jones."

"I know who you are."

Jobyna held out the package. "Just a little something I saw and thought you might like."

Martha looked from the offered package to Jobyna's face.

"Open it, please," Jobyna said.

Martha handed the skillet to Lily, took the gift, untied the ribbon, tore off the paper, and opened the box. Inside was a bright red silk scarf, hand-painted with a floral design. Martha ran her hand across the soft fabric and held it to her cheek.

"Look how beautiful that color is against her skin, Lily. Here."
Jobyna draped the scarf around Martha's neck and stood back to
admire her. "Perfect. The ladies in church are sure going to envy you."

Martha smiled and held open the screen door. "We were about to
have our supper. Have you had yours?"

Jobyna winked at Lily and followed Martha into the house.

Carl and the two boys took their seats at the kitchen table. Martha
insisted that Jobyna take the place of honor at the head of the table and
that Lily sit to her right instead of helping Martha serve the meal. "Sit
here and visit with your friend," Martha said.

After supper, Martha shooed them out of the kitchen into the living
room. The boys were full of questions about Jobyna's experiences
traveling around the South in her own railroad car.

"Don't bother Miz Jones, boys," Carl said. "Let her relax."

"I don't mind." She told the boys stories that Lily had never heard
before, about how she started singing at nine years old for loose change
on street corners in Chattanooga, how she and her band rode and slept
in a wagon drawn by mules as they went from show to show when she
was getting started, and how she was finally able to buy and outfit her
railroad car. "I'll show you my car sometime, boys." She turned to Lily.
"I'd like to go into town and see what's gone on since I've been here
last. Will you ride with me, Lily?"

Lily ran to change out of her cotton house dress and to get her hat.

In the back seat of the Duesenberg, Jobyna pulled Lily onto her lap
and kissed her. She caught the driver's eye in the mirror. "Take us to
town to Ace's Place, Ray. I need a drink." She closed the privacy screen
between the front and back seat.

***

Lily had ridden a bus and had walked down Market Street in
Chattanooga, but she had never glided down the street in a flashy
yellow car. In the gathering twilight, people on the sidewalk stopped to
stare and wave as they passed. She felt pride sitting in the backseat
holding hands with Jobyna Jones, the Empress of Blues. She stole a
sideways look at Jobyna, staring out the car window and puffing on a
cigarette through her ebony cigarette holder. Lily waited for Jobyna to
talk about their future as she had in her letter, about the house they
would have together in Atlanta.

The car slowed as they approached a two-story brick building with a sign that said, "John F. Fischer Family Funeral Home" and underneath, "We Grieve With You." The driver steered the car into an alley beside the building and stopped halfway down in front of a metal door that was once painted red but had faded to a shade of rust.

The driver left the motor running and went to the door. He knocked and spoke a few words that Lily couldn't make out to someone behind a peephole. The driver stepped back around the car, opened Jobyna's door, and nodded.

Jobyna kissed Lily and helped her from the car. "Let's go, baby."

The metal door swung open. A huge black man came forward to catch Jobyna up in a bear hug. He seemed to Lily to be seven feet tall and to weigh as much as two men. His tailor-made suit fitted him perfectly. He smiled at Jobyna, and the light over the door reflected off several gold teeth. "Get in here, gal. We haven't seen you in a month of Sundays. We haven't had any fun at all, just waiting for you to come back."

Jobyna chuckled. "Hello, Ace. I see Lola hasn't stopped feeding you."

Ace guffawed and patted his barrel chest. "Naw. But you know what they say...being fat is God's way of saying, 'You're so good I think that I'll make more of you.'"

"Go on, Ace." Jobyna took Lily's hand. "This is Lily."

"Delighted, Miz Lily." Ace bowed and touched the brim of an imaginary hat. "Ya'll come in. I've got you a special table."

He held the door while Jobyna led Lily down some wooden stairs into a smoky barroom not yet full this early in the evening. It seemed to Lily that everyone there recognized Jobyna. They crowded around to shake her hand and pat her on the back. This was the blues singer's life, and it would be her life, too, when they were together. She stood on the sidelines while Jobyna spoke to every well-wisher. Ace led the two of them to a table directly in front of a small stage where four musicians were setting up their instruments. He brought a bottle and two glasses on a tray.

Jobyna filled their glasses. "Sorry, baby, about all that to-do."

"I don't mind. They love you is all." She looked into Jobyna's eyes. "And I do, too."

Jobyna took a long drink of the amber liquid. "I have to talk to you about something, Lily."

Lily held her breath. From Jobyna's tone, what she had to talk about wasn't good news for Lily. To calm herself, she sat very still, focusing on the musicians.

"Look at me, baby." Jobyna took Lily's chin in her hand. "I know you're going to be disappointed, but I didn't come to Chattanooga to get you. I came to tell you that we have to wait a little while longer. I'm not going to stay in Atlanta. Little T's not satisfied with what the radio station is offering. He thinks they're trying to take advantage of us, so we're going to New York City instead. He says we can get a Columbia Records recording contract."

Tears of frustration burned behind Lily's eyes, but she struggled to maintain her composure. "Don't you want me to go with you to New York?"

"Of course, I do. I want you with me, and I'll send for you as soon as I can. We can still have the house we talked about, just in New York instead of Atlanta."

Lily looked at her hands in her lap without responding.

"You believe me, don't you, baby? You can see I need to get things lined up first. We were right to wait about Atlanta, as it turned out." Jobyna lit another cigarette, tossed back her drink, and poured herself another.

"What makes you think Little T will be any better at making a record deal than he was with the radio people? I can tell he doesn't want you having anything to do with me. Maybe he's keeping us apart on purpose."

"You let me worry about Little T. I know he thinks he tells me what to do, but I make my own life. If you'll just bear with me, I'll send you a bus ticket as soon as I can, or maybe you'd rather come on the train. It won't be any longer than another two or three weeks. I promise." Jobyna caressed Lily's thigh under the table, sending a chill through her body.

"I know what. We'll go to the train station right now and buy you a ticket. You wait here. I've got a little business to take care of with Ace, then we'll go."

Jobyna patted Lily's hand and went over to Ace, who was showing two couples to a table by the bar. Lily watched Jobyna whisper something to him. He nodded, and the two of them went through a door beside the bar. Jobyna came out a few minutes later holding a thick manila envelope. She started back toward their table and paused to speak to some patrons on her way.

"Do you want another drink or are you ready to go?" she asked when she got back to Lily.

Lily shook her head. "Let's go. What's in the envelope?"

"Ace was holding some money for me. We're going to need it for our New York house. Let's go get your train ticket."

Chapter Thirteen

MARTHA'S CARDBOARD FAN, WITH a picture of a white Jesus walking in the Garden of Gethsemane, swished rhythmically in time with the choir's weekly special musical selection. Every other fan stroke stirred the still, heavy air in Lily's direction. She shifted her weight in her spot on the pine pew between Martha and one of her nephews.

As the last chord on the old upright piano faded, the preacher rose to stand behind the pulpit and deliver his sermon. Lily welcomed this time of the week. For an hour and a half, or sometimes two, she could fix her gaze on the minister as though she was listening with rapt attention and daydream uninterrupted about Jobyna and when they would be together in New York City.

Today was the fourth Sunday since Jobyna came to Chattanooga to tell Lily about her move to New York. Lily got three or four letters from Jobyna every week. Each letter started out describing the marvels Jobyna saw in the big city and giving optimistic reports about Little T's progress on a contract with Columbia Records. The letter always ended with melancholy refrains about how much she missed Lily and hopeful plans about the time they could be together, but there wasn't any talk of when that might be. Jobyna described the rooming house where they were staying in Harlem, but she had no set address, so Lily wrote Jobyna everyday care of General Delivery, hoping that the letters somehow found their way to her.

She kept Jobyna's letters and the train ticket in a cigar box at the bottom of the one bureau drawer Martha was able to spare her. When she lost hope that the day would ever come that they would be together, she pulled out the cigar box and read each letter. She ran her fingers across the train ticket to make sure it was real.

The preacher's voice, raised in the booming climax of his sermon, roused Lily from her daydreaming. The choir began the invitational hymn. The pastor invited the members of the congregation to come to the altar to confess their sins and witness to their family and neighbors how they planned to do better during the coming week. The preacher didn't waste much time on this part of the service. No one ever came forward for a public confession. Was the preacher disappointed or relieved? He walked down the center aisle reciting the closing prayer, and then took his place at the front door to shake hands with the departing congregation.

Martha shooed her boys and Lily toward the door with Carl trailing behind. "We have to hurry. Carl's cousin Arthur from Jasper is coming on the train to Sunday dinner, and I have to get the chicken on the stove."

Lily knew who Arthur Greene was. She had seen him in Jasper occasionally as she was growing up, but he was older. He went away to the War when Lily was in seventh or eighth grade. Her memory was of a tall, lanky boy, his wrists and ankles showing beyond sleeves and pant legs as his clothes couldn't keep up with his growth. Carl spoke fondly of him. He admired Arthur's business success. He left their family's traditional pathway of farming to work in a Jasper grocery store. After the war, he came back to be manager. He eventually bought the store from the aging owner.

"Arthur don't ever have to worry about whether it rains or not or whether the boll weevils get into the cotton crop. He just sets back and waits for people to come in and buy groceries. People got to eat, no matter what."

By the time the family walked the half mile home from church, Arthur was already there, sitting on the edge of the front porch. As they came into the yard, Arthur jumped up and removed his hat. He shook hands with Carl, made a courtly bow to Martha and Lily, and then ruffled the twins' hair.

Lily was surprised by Arthur's looks. In the years since Lily saw him stocking shelves and bagging groceries in the store, he had matured. She supposed it was his time in the War in France that changed his looks. He filled out his black Sunday suit, and the sleeves and pant legs fit. The shirt underneath, buttoned all the way up to the top, was gleaming white and showed off his broad chest.

Martha and Lily bustled into the kitchen to prepare the fried chicken, mashed potatoes, green peas, cornbread, and apple pie that were the standard menu for their Sunday dinner, and Martha put the boys to work setting the table. Out the back-screen door, Lily watched Carl and Arthur walk side by side down rows of cotton plants, Carl pointing out details of the crop and Arthur nodding with his hands in his pockets.

Martha spooned lard into the iron skillet and began dredging the chicken pieces in flour. She glanced sideways at Lily. "He's single, you know."

Lily moved away from the door to finish cutting up the potatoes. "I wonder why he is still. He'd look like a catch to most girls."

"But not to you?"

"No, not to me."

Martha shook her head without commenting. As the chicken popped and sizzled in the hot grease, Martha called to the men and the two boys to wash up for the meal. The family found their seats. Carl said a blessing over the food and began to pass the plates around the table. Martha made sure that Arthur got first pick of the meat as he was the honored guest.

After dinner, Lily and Arthur sat alone on the porch swing. In the living room, the boys argued good-naturedly over a card game. Martha and Carl had disappeared, and Lily wasn't sure where they had gone, but she was sure it was a deliberate move to leave Arthur and her alone together. Did Arthur notice? She felt a little embarrassed and uncomfortable.

Arthur rocked the swing. A breeze passed over and rustled the waist-high cotton plants. "You don't remember me from Jasper days, do you?"

"Of course." She glanced at Arthur. "I remember you nearly drowned me once."

"What? I don't remember anything like that."

"I was about eleven or twelve, I guess. A bunch of us were floating on inner tubes in the river. You swam up to me, grabbed hold of my inner tube, and asked me if I could swim. I couldn't swim a lick, but I said I could anyway. Then you turned me smack over, and I sank like a rock. I wasn't even struggling, I just thought, 'Well, this is the way it feels when you drown.' You grabbed me around the waist and pulled me up to the surface. It scared you to death. The look on your face was so shocked, I just had to laugh."

"That's awful. I don't remember it at all. I do remember wanting to get you to notice me. Guess I did that, but not the way I had in mind."

"After that I would see you in the grocery store, but you never spoke to me again. Then I guess you went away to the War."

"Yes. I thought they needed me to win." Arthur laughed. "I lied about my age; I was only sixteen."

The boys burst through the screen door, interrupting the two on the swing. Arthur chuckled and looked after the two boys as they jumped off the porch, one chasing the other full speed down the gravel road. Arthur leaned forward with his elbows on his knees, and the sleeves of his white shirt rode up, showing his wrists that were still oddly delicate in spite of his maturing since their younger days.

"I heard you been living the high life here lately, traveling and on the stage. You must think we're dull after all that. Most people around here have never even been to a stage show, let alone acted in one. We have tent shows come through Jasper every so often, but that's way different, I guess."

Lily shook her head but didn't go on about her life over the last few months. Her time with Jobyna and her hopes about the future were a secret she didn't want to share with Arthur or Martha or anyone. She might be tempting fate if she told her dreams out loud. She did have to admit that Arthur was easy to talk to. He was very still when she talked, listening to her with what seemed to be genuine interest.

"Did you go to France during the War?"

"Yes, to a place they call Lorraine. In the south."

"Were you afraid?"

Arthur blew out a breath and rubbed his forehead. "I was at first. But it turned out I was just a supply clerk. They didn't let us fight with the white boys. Besides, I got there at the very end. It was almost over before I could even turn around."

"Did you learn to speak French?"

"*Oui.*"

Lily waited for more.

"*Oui.* That's about it."

Lily thought about the funny little man in their rooming house in New Orleans who spoke Creole French and kissed Jobyna behind each ear. That memory made her think of Jobyna, as she did obsessively several times an hour. She pictured her leaning back on her elbows on Lily's bed in the fancy rooming house in New Orleans, smiling as Lily tried on the beautiful white dress.

The twins came marching back up the gravel road, their arms around each other's shoulders. They climbed the porch steps, heavy work shoes clomping in unison across the boards and into the house.

"So, you came back to Chattanooga."

Lily nodded. "But not to stay."

"I was hoping I could see more of you. I promise not to try to drown you, even if you tell me to go away and leave me alone."

"I'm going to New York City. Maybe in just a few days."

"For another show?"

"No. I was not a very good dancer."

When Lily put Arthur off about his interest in her, she expected that he would find a reason to say goodbye to her and the family as quickly as he could and head into town for the train back to Jasper. Instead, he seemed to relax once the pressure of courting Lily was off. He leaned back in the swing and stretched out his legs.

"After the War, I never wanted to be anywhere but Jasper." He glanced over at Lily. "Now that's boring, isn't it?"

Lily shrugged. She hoped her indifference wasn't rude, but she was anxious to be on her own to find a private place to re-read Jobyna's letters and think about when they would be together.

At last Arthur seemed to take the hint. He slapped his knees and stood up, straightened his pant legs, and stuck his hands in his pockets. "I'll get started back." But he apparently wasn't ready to give up on Lily. "I was thinking...next Sunday, if you're still here and haven't gone to New York, I could come and get you. We could ride the train to Jasper. I want you to see my store. You remember the diner on the square that serves Sunday dinner? Not as good as Martha's cooking, but almost. Consider it me making up for almost drowning you."

"Maybe." Lily had no interest but didn't have the heart to be rude.

"Good. I'll come for sure. You can decide about going to Jasper in the meantime." Arthur said his goodbyes to Martha and Carl and the boys and struck out on foot toward town to catch the train.

Chapter Fourteen

A WEEK LATER, CARL declared the fields were ready for harvest. The boys' school let out especially for cotton picking. Lily and Martha joined them in the field during the day, each dragging eight-foot cotton sacks between the rows of white bolls. Lily didn't mind the work. Carl paid her by the pound, based on how much her sack weighed at the end of the day. The mindless mechanics of pulling the tufts of cotton from the prickly bolls and filling her sack allowed her uninterrupted daydreams about Jobyna or time to chat with Martha as they moved down the rows. Martha was more practiced and faster with picking, but she sometimes held back a little to let Lily stay even with her.

Martha stood up straight, stretched her back, and wiped her forehead with the back of her hand. She glanced over her shoulder at Lily. "How was your visit yesterday with Arthur in Jasper?"

"It was fine. Jasper's...Jasper. It seems like a hundred years since I left there, but the place looks exactly the same. Same folks walking on Main Street. They let colored people in the diner on the square now. I guess that changed some with the War and all. We have to go in the back door and pick up our food through a little window in the kitchen, but it's the same food the white folks eat."

"Did he show you his store?"

"He's very proud of it. He's left the old sign up, the one that says Gable's Grocery. I suspect most people don't know he's the owner and not still just the manager."

Martha pulled cotton bolls for a while in silence. "He's a good man, Arthur."

Martha seemed to be fishing for some encouragement that Lily might consider him more than a friend. "Mmm-hmm," Lily said. She stood and gauged how close to full her cotton sack might be. "Should we get Carl to weigh us out and head home to start supper?"

After the meal, Lily went out to the pump to draw dishwater while Martha cleared the supper things. Would Martha miss her when she went to New York? Her staying with the family in the small house was more work for her sister, in a way, but she hoped she was good company for Martha. The routine of daily life in Chattanooga had been good for Lily, too. It kept her from obsessing too much about Jobyna.

She pulled her sweater close with one hand, hooked the water bucket over the pump spout, and began moving the pump handle up and down. It seemed the weather had turned overnight. Last week the evenings had been warm, but tonight a chill wind blew across the cotton field and tugged at her skirt.

She lugged the full bucket across the back porch and into the kitchen and put the water on the stove to heat up while she helped Martha clear the table. She heard Carl settle heavily into his easy chair in the living room and snap open the newspaper. She pictured him carefully folding it in quarters and pushing his reading glasses up on his nose. Then she heard the scrape of his thick-soled work shoes as he stood quickly and came to the kitchen door.

"Lily, isn't this your friend?" He held the paper out to her.

She shifted the dishes she was holding to one hand and took the paper. It was a close-up photograph of Jobyna in a white turban holding an ostrich feather fan and staring seductively into the camera lens. Lily recognized the picture from a publicity poster advertising the traveling show. The headline read, "Local Singer Shot and Killed in New York City Speakeasy."

Lily threw the newspaper against the wall. She heard a high, keening cry that seemed to come from somewhere outside, then a crash as the dishes she was holding hit the floor, then a thud as she fell to her knees on top of them.

"What in the world?" Martha ran over and pulled Lily to her feet. "Look at these dishes, and your knees are bleeding." Martha looked from Lily to Carl. "What is it?"

"It's the paper." Carl picked up the newspaper from the floor and showed Martha the picture and headline.

"Set her down and get her a glass of water while I see to her knees." Martha's voice sounded very far away. Lily felt a sensation that was vaguely familiar, and then she remembered. It felt like the time Arthur turned over her inner tube, and she was sinking in the river.

Chapter Fifteen

SHE WOKE THE NEXT morning in the boys' bed. Martha had wrapped clean cotton rags around her knees to stop her bleeding from the cuts. Lily went into the empty kitchen and found a cold biscuit left over from breakfast and poured a cup of tepid coffee. Out the back door she saw Martha bent over a row, dragging a cotton sack.

Lily pulled on her work clothes, keeping her back turned to the newspaper that Carl had left on his chair in the living room, and went out. The slam of the screen door made Martha pause and look toward the house, shielding her eyes from the sun. "Lily, you don't need to come out today. Stay in and let your knees heal up some."

Lily hooked the strap of her cotton sack over one shoulder and bent at the start of a row.

"Well, wait a minute and I'll pick with you till we're even. Did you eat some breakfast?"

Lily worked all day alongside Martha, and then helped with supper and the dishes. Carl read another article about the murder. At first, he began to read the article aloud to Lily, but she found a way to keep busy in the kitchen to avoid hearing it. As she dried the supper dishes, she told herself that it was some terrible case of mistaken identity, and that if she just refused to listen, it wouldn't be true.

The family went to bed, and the only sound was the katydids' chirping outside. Lily stared sleepless into the dark, seized with anger at herself. If she had only insisted on going to New York with Jobyna, she could have convinced her to stay away from Little T and this wouldn't have happened. Little T was dangerous. He carried a gun. Jobyna might not have even gone to that speakeasy where she got shot if Lily had been with her. She buried her head in the pillow and sobbed silently with helpless frustration.

At church on Sunday, instead of daydreaming about being with Jobyna as she usually did, Lily prayed. She promised God that if he would turn back time and make Jobyna still alive, she would give her up. "If my love for her is a sin, you can strike me dead instead." But God didn't strike her dead, and the preacher said the final prayer, and the family went home to Sunday fried chicken dinner as usual.

On Monday morning, Martha couldn't rouse Lily from the couch where she slept. It wasn't in Martha's nature to dwell on the emotions that might overtake someone or to spend time puzzling over the mystery of why Jobyna's death had such a profound effect on Lily, but facts were facts. Lily had shut down. That night, Martha moved the boys quasi-permanently into the living room to sleep on the floor on a pallet made of quilts and gave Lily their bedroom. The rest of the week, she hand-fed her sister in bed after the family finished their meals. If she hadn't, Lily would simply have given up eating. Martha made Lily sit up so that she could wash her face and body with a warm washcloth. She peeked in on Lily as she went about her work during the day, and often found her asleep or weeping softly into the pillow.

Carl worried that they should be doing something to try and console her. Lily overheard Carl ask Martha in the kitchen, "Don't you think she needs to know what happened? Maybe that will help her come to terms with it. I saved all the articles that the newspaper printed."

Lily heard Martha murmured an unintelligible answer, which was quickly followed by Carl's soft knock on the bedroom door. She wasn't sure she could bear hearing the details of Jobyna's death, but she was upsetting Carl's life and family with her tragedy, so she let Carl read the articles to her. The *Chattanooga Times* ran stories every day for a week about Jobyna's death in the Harlem night club. Jobyna's hometown celebrity added to the public's natural fascination with a drama that could have been a movie script. The paper sent a reporter all the way from Chattanooga to New York to interview eyewitnesses who were only too happy to supply all the lurid details.

A barmaid said she saw the whole thing. Jobyna and Little T were drinking with a white record company big shot and his girlfriend. Around midnight, the club was full of customers, and a shouting match broke out between Little T and Jobyna. It appeared to be about her paying too much attention to one or the other of the couple. Little T ordered her to leave with him and grabbed her by the arm. Jobyna said something that made the white couple laugh, and Little T pulled a gun from his waistband and shot her. Little T dropped the gun and ran toward the street, but a bouncer at the front door tackled him. Someone called the police and an ambulance, but it was too late for Jobyna.

The most recent article said that Little T was in jail without bail and quoted a guard saying that he kept mumbling about doing away with himself, but that no one took him very seriously. "A man that would shoot a woman like that? He's a coward and not likely to hang himself in here. Good riddance if he did, you ask me."

Carl folded the last newspaper and took off his reading glasses. He hugged Lily and let her sob against his shoulder.

The next morning, Lily got up and dressed and helped Martha fix breakfast for Carl and the boys. She joined the family again in the cotton field.

Chapter Sixteen

LILY STOOD ON TIPTOES to hand the strap of her picking sack to Carl so that he could haul it up to be weighed and emptied. He was standing in the bed of the wagon, knee-deep in cotton.

"This is the last sack of the year, Lily. I don't know what we'd have done without you to help with the picking. It wasn't near as glamorous as dancing in a traveling show, but we've sure been glad to have you." Carl jumped down and began hitching the two mules to the wagon. "The boys and I will get this last load over to the gin. You'll want to go get cleaned up, I guess. Arthur's coming again tonight, isn't he?"

Lily nodded.

"I'm glad to see you two getting along so well. That Arthur is a fine fellow."

She was just going through the motions of living. She could usually keep herself busy enough to put Jobyna out of her mind for spurts of time, but as often as she could she found a way to be alone with Jobyna's letters and the train ticket that she would never use.

Arthur must have noticed her distance, but he never let on. He traveled to the farm every Sunday for dinner, and sometimes, like tonight, he came on Saturday after he closed the grocery store. There were times when Lily couldn't bring herself to come out of the kitchen. Arthur never complained. He spent those times talking with Carl and the twins and came into the kitchen only to say goodbye to Lily before heading back to Jasper.

Last week he told Lily, "I have a surprise for you next Saturday night." Lily pretended she was interested. Arthur was kind, and so eager to please her. And as Carl said, he was a fine fellow and owned a successful business. She couldn't stay on with Martha and Carl much longer. Now that the crop was in, it would be even more awkward for her to stay.

She hurried back to the house, washed up, and changed her dress. She heard the rattle of a car engine as a Model T parked next to the front porch. The engine coughed twice and stopped. What was the mailman doing stopping in their yard? Could it be another letter from Jobyna? But then reality came rushing back. There would be no more

79

letters.

Lily went to the door and watched Arthur climb from behind the steering wheel and pause to polish a spot on the fender with his sleeve. He wore a new suit with a vest and a bow tie—fancier than the black Sunday suit he usually wore—and a fedora set on his head at a jaunty angle. He saw Lily standing at the door, and grinned. "How do you like her?"

"Where did you get it? Is that the surprise?"

"It's part of the surprise. I bought it. Man's got to have a car nowadays." He pulled a folded piece of paper from his pocket, opened it with a flourish, and handed it to Lily. "This is the rest of the surprise." It was an advertisement for a traveling tent show in Jasper that night. Across the top in big red letters the flyer said, "Tonight...the King Oliver Creole Jazz Band." There was a photograph of Oliver blowing his cornet in front of five other band members in tuxedos. Lower down on the page there was a smaller photo of a woman seated in front of a painted palm tree and smiling into the camera lens. The flyer read, "Featuring the South's newest blues sensation...Ruth Flame."

"Arthur, this is Ruth, my cousin!"

Arthur chuckled. "I know."

Lily ran into the kitchen to show the flyer to Martha. "Charlie Reed really came through on his promise."

Martha wiped her hands on her apron and took the paper. "Who's Charlie Reed?"

"It doesn't matter. But, look. They're letting Ruth sing, just like she's always dreamed she would."

***

The big tent glowed yellow against a cloudless night sky. Red, white, and blue flags fluttered from the tent poles that made peaks in the top. A trail of kerosene lamps led the crowd across the newly plowed-under field to the front entrance. Arthur took Lily's elbow as they wound between automobiles and empty cotton wagons with teams of mules grazing on stubble.

The place was full of men and women dressed in their Sunday best, already clapping along with the music of King Oliver and the band. Arthur and Lily were lucky to find seats close to the front as the line of chorus girls tapped onto the stage.

Arthur leaned over to whisper in Lily's ear. "Is this what you did on the tour?"

Lily nodded. She was sitting on the edge of her seat, anticipating Ruth taking the stage. The band played the chorus line off the stage after their number and swung through their rendition of "Riverside Blues" that had the crowd dancing in the aisles. Then they struck up the intro to "Downhearted Blues," one of Jobyna's standards. Lily held her breath as Ruth came strutting out from the wing dressed in a red sequined dress, her arms draped with a red feather boa. The crowd roared their approval. Ruth stepped to the edge of the stage, just behind the kerosene footlights.

Lily remembered Ruth the night of the Nashville show, peeking at Jobyna from behind the stage curtain and mouthing her words and mimicking her gestures. Tonight, Ruth did a good job of making the tune her own, and the audience loved her, demanding three encores.

After the show, Arthur led Lily behind the big tent to a smaller one that was serving as a dressing room for the women performers. Ruth squealed and threw herself at Lily, twirling her around in a circle. Lily pulled Arthur forward. "Ruth, this is Arthur Greene. You might remember him from Jasper."

Ruth stepped back and eyed Arthur. "Not the Arthur from Mr. Gable's grocery store?"

Arthur looked nervously around the small tent full of girls in various stages of undress and fidgeted with his hat. "I'm that Arthur. Lily, I'll wait outside while you and Ruth visit."

Ruth glanced around the dressing tent and moved Lily over to a corner, away from the crowd of women. She hugged Lily again. "I'm so sorry about Jobyna. I heard she was up in New York when it happened. I thought you might have been with her, but I guess not. I'm glad of that."

"No, I'm staying with Martha and Carl. Oh, Ruth. Don't you think I could have stopped it?"

Ruth shook her head. "No, he would just have shot you, too. He was never going to let Jobyna get away from him. Now he'll go to the electric chair for it."

Lily didn't want to talk about Jobyna's death with Ruth and risk breaking down in tears. "Now you're Ruth Flame."

"Yes. Do you like my stage name?"

"Very fancy. It looks like Charlie Reed kept his promise."

Ruth made a face and looked like she wanted to spit on the sawdust floor but was restraining herself. "Charlie Reed didn't do a thing for me. I sat in a room in a New Orleans boarding house for days waiting for him to use his so-called 'great connections' to get me into another show. All he had was one excuse after another. You were so right about him. Thank goodness I ran into Max one night. You remember Max, the director of Jobyna's show?"

"Yes." Lily remembered the baleful stares Max used to give her and her fear that he would throw her off the stage and out of Jobyna's show.

"I was blowing the last of my bonus money from Jobyna on dinner at Antoine's. Max was there with King Oliver. They were leaving the next day for a tent show tour of the South. Tent shows are getting to be more popular than theater shows. Cheaper to put together, and you can go to places that don't have a music hall like the big cities. It doesn't hurt that Mr. Oliver gets to keep all the profit, too. He doesn't have to share with a theater owner after T-O-B-A takes their cut off the top.

"Anyway, their girl singer ran off with some Johnny at the last minute, and they were thinking they'd have to do without vocals on the tour. I told them I might be able to arrange my schedule to go with them. Just a minor exaggeration. Max vouched for me, and Mr. Oliver let me get up right in the restaurant and try out. He liked what he saw and heard, and I left with them on the bus the next morning."

Lily glanced at Arthur standing outside the open tent flap, gazing up at the sky with his hands in his pockets. He was softly whistling "Downhearted Blues" off-key. It made her smile.

"Come with us, Lily,"

"What?"

"I can talk them into letting you come with us. We're going to Knoxville next. They don't need any more dancers, but you can be my dresser. I can afford to pay you some, and you can room with me." Ruth took Lily's hands in hers. "You don't have anything holding you here, do you?"

Lily looked out at Arthur again. "I think I might have someone holding me here."

PART TWO

1964

JOBIE

Chapter Seventeen

JOBIE GREENE STRUGGLED TO swing open the heavy metal door, juggling her duffel bag and guitar case. She paused just inside the barn-like room to get her bearings and tried to push her hair back out of her eyes with her shoulder. That failed, and she set the duffel down with a thump to smooth the cowlick at the hairline of her dark, pencil-straight hair.

Jobie was relieved as she looked around the cavernous studio filled with cameras, cables, and lights. When the boxy black car lurched away from the curb at Heathrow airport outside London, she hadn't been sure that the taxi driver knew where he was going. He repeated, "Associated British Corporation Studios," but then he said something that sounded like "Teddington." She crossed her fingers and hoped for the best.

Across the studio, a technician was working over a sound board. He glanced up at her but went back to work without comment. She took a few steps toward him and cleared her throat. "Excuse me. Is this the studio for *Thank Your Lucky Stars*?"

"The very same," he answered. "And if you're looking for the producer, you'll find her with Deedee on the set around the corner. You'll recognize which one is the producer. She'll be the nervous-looking one with the clipboard."

Jobie picked up her bag and walked around a prop canvas wall. A woman with shaggy-cut short brown hair, holding a clipboard, was standing in front of a metal scaffold, looking up at another woman perched at the top. Her hair was platinum blond and the color seemed to pulsate under the stage lights. She wore black stirrup pants, an oversized black shirt, and silver pixie boots.

"Deedee, be reasonable." The producer paced in front of the scaffold. "Everyone does it. The Beatles, Cilla, everyone. You know the skimpy budget I have to work with."

"I don't care what everyone does, and I don't care about your budget, Kate," the woman on the scaffold said. "I don't lip-synch. It's not what these kids come to see, and it makes me look and feel like an idiot. So, figure it out." She flung the musical score she was holding in the direction of the producer, and Jobie watched as pages fluttered down like falling leaves. One page landed on Jobie's chest, and she set down her guitar case quickly to catch the paper.

The platinum haired woman climbed athletically down the scaffold and headed toward Jobie. "Sorry." She took the score page from Jobie and glanced over her shoulder at the producer who was gathering up the pages off the floor. "Sometimes you just have to get her attention." She offered her hand. "I'm Deedee O'Gwinn."

"Jobie Greene."

"Jobie?" Deedee leaned in to make sure she'd heard correctly.

"Yes, short for Jobyna."

"Like Jobyna Jones?" the two women said in unison.

"Yes." Jobie laughed, surprised that this English woman in 1964 knew of the 1920s' American blues singer. "I'm named after her. My grandmother traveled with her show in the twenties. As a dancer."

Deedee nodded. "Deedee is short for Dorothy Delia. Back In the sixth grade, I told the nuns that I would grow up to be a blues singer. You should have seen their faces when I belted out 'St. Louis Blues' at the All Saints Celebration. So, am I right, you're American?" She eyed the guitar case. "And are you a blues singer like Jobyna Jones?"

"Yes, I'm American, but not a blues singer. I wouldn't be very believable singing the blues. I haven't paid any dues."

"You mean no one's broken your heart yet."

Jobie shook her head. "No, and I'm not looking for that to happen anytime soon."

Deedee's eyes sparkled, and she smiled a little. "Well, you better be on the lookout. You never know when they're going to show up."

The producer interrupted. "You win, Deedee, but only because it's you. I'm going to call in some session musicians. You can rehearse with them tomorrow morning. If you want Marilyn and the girls to come in for backup, you'll have to pay for them yourself. There I draw the line." She shoved the score in Deedee's chest.

"Oh, thank you, luv." She gave the producer a quick hug. "Jobie Greene, this is Kate Castle, the best TV producer around who gets far too little credit from all the suits at the network." Kate acknowledged the compliment with a wave and hurried over to a telephone in the corner of the studio.

"So." Deedee turned back to Jobie. "You were telling me about your music. Not a blues singer. What are you?"

"Folk. I sing Dylan, Woody Guthrie, and some of my own. I don't do much television, mostly coffee houses and studio recordings, mostly in New York. This whole trip was my record label's brainchild. They have some idea about opening up the UK market more to folk music."

Deedee reached up and touched Jobie's cheek so softly that, even though caught off-guard, Jobie didn't flinch. "They have the right idea about putting this face on TV. The colors of your eyes and skin are amazing. You'll be a great contrast to all us pale-faced English types."

Before Jobie could respond, a loud *whoomp* sounded, and the bank of lights on the stage went dark. Three more *whoomps* in quick succession darkened the entire studio, leaving only the orange exit signs glowing.

"What just happened?" Jobie asked.

"Don't worry, luv, it's the afternoon tea break for all the crafts people. Union requires it. Everything will be back on in half an hour. I've got to run and get my singers together. See you at the show tomorrow night?" Without waiting for a reply, Deedee turned and hurried away toward one of the exit signs.

Jobie stood in the dark studio looking after her and replaying the relationship advice. What made Deedee, who she figured was about her age, such an expert on heartbreak? And she made it sound as though heartbreak was inevitable, or even a good thing. Jobie wasn't ready to believe she had to suffer to be a successful singer.

She spent the rest of the afternoon going over her cues with Kate and running through the two numbers she planned for the show. She chose a Dylan protest song, "Masters of War," thinking that the crowd of young Brits would expect that from an American folk singer, though Jobie thought of herself as an entertainer, not a political activist. She sometimes felt guilty about her lack of passion about political causes.

She had once approached Bob Dylan at the Gaslight Club in Greenwich Village. Jobie was at the very beginning of her career and Dylan was headlining at the club. She was hanging around, trying to get a fifteen-minute gig in the afternoon. She asked him where he got his inspiration for the lyrics of his protest songs. He said, "I only write what I think people want to hear." She felt better after that. He didn't sound like some guru genius on a remote mountaintop. Maybe even she would develop passion for causes as she grew older and more experienced.

Her other song for the TV show would be "Puff the Magic Dragon." The tune was always a crowd-pleaser. The audience liked to sing along. Since she would be accompanying herself on her guitar, there was no need for an emotional scene with the producer—like Deedee's—over whether to sing live or lip-synch.

"We go out live at seven, so be here at five sharp for hair and makeup," Kate said. "That will put you ahead of Deedee in the makeup chair. She's a perfectionist and—" Kate caught herself mid-sentence and ran her hand through her short hair. "I'll just say that she takes a long time in the makeup chair."

Jobie waited for her to continue, curious to know more about Deedee. Kate turned away without going on, and Jobie ventured a comment. "She seems formidable."

"Oh, she is that, and an amazing talent, too."

"Tell me more about her. I'm not that familiar with British popular music, sorry to say."

Kate didn't respond right away. She looked down at her clipboard and adjusted the papers. "If you want to know more about Deedee, ask her yourself."

Jobie backed up a step. She had clearly offended the producer in some unknown way. "Sorry."

"Just be here on time for makeup." Kate hurried off to confer with the lighting tech.

***

Jobie arrived back at the studio at five o'clock sharp the next evening. By 5:30, the makeup girl pronounced her done. She found the dressing room that she would share with the female acts who were set to appear that evening. She took out her guitar and tuned it, softly strumming through the two numbers she would sing on the show. She placed her guitar carefully back in its case and sat drumming her fingers, looking around the cramped space.

Deedee had apparently been in already that day. The top of a vanity was covered with pots of creams, lipsticks, eyeliner, and mascara. There was a clothes rack along one wall with a dozen dresses on hangers, half of them pink and the other half yellow. On a shelf above the dresses sat three platinum-blond wigs on mannequin heads, curled and ratted into intricate hairdos.

Jobie stood up and looked at herself in the full-length mirror that hung on the back of the dressing room door. She wore straight-legged jeans, a blousy white linen shirt, and sandals. If makeup, beehive hairdos, and frilly dresses were what these British kids expected, they were certainly going to see something different with Jobie. She stepped closer to the mirror. Deedee had said her looks were "amazing" for TV. She studied her own reflection: dark hair and eyes, even features, and coffee-with-cream skin inherited from the combination of genes from her African American mother and white father.

She turned around, looked over her shoulder in the mirror, and gathered up the tail of her blouse. Not a bad figure. She giggled aloud, imagining Deedee saying, "That ass will look amazing on TV."

Jobie heard voices and laughter in the hallway outside the door, and before she could move, the dressing room door opened on Deedee and three other women carrying more frilly dresses and high-heeled shoes. Jobie stood frozen with her blouse pulled up and her butt stuck out.

"Very nice, if you're looking for a critique."

"I guess I was critiquing myself." Jobie stepped away from the mirror. "All your costumes and wigs and makeup are making me wonder how I'll come across with these kids. As I told you, I'm used to audiences in coffee houses in Greenwich Village, not TV studios in London."

Deedee took Jobie's chin in her hand and turned her face to the mirror. "You look exotic, like a folk singer should. Made up, I look like a pop singer. We're both playing our roles." She stood for a moment smiling into their reflection before turning to the three backup singers. "Girls, this is the American I was telling you about."

Jobie felt a little thrill of pleasure that Deedee had been thinking about her and had mentioned her to the backup singers.

"Jobie, this is Marilyn, Peggy, and Betty. They'll be backing me up tonight, and we need to get a move on."

At seven o'clock sharp, the bouncy *Thank Your Lucky Stars* theme music filled the studio. Jobie watched an oddly proper middle-aged master of ceremonies with a handheld microphone introduce the show. A sea of two hundred young men and women packing the cramped set shoulder to shoulder bobbed up and down in time with the music.

The master of ceremonies introduced the first act, a four-man singing group called Freddie and the Dreamers. They wore the Merseybeat uniform of the day: skinny black suits with white shirts, narrow neckties, and boots with Cuban heels. Their act featured a lead singer, Freddie, who stood not much over five feet and bounced around the stage with arms and legs flying as the band lip-synched and pretended to play an upbeat tune about young love among the birds singing and bees humming.

The girls in the audience grabbed Freddie's sleeves and ruffled his hair playfully. After their number, the second host, a girl with long, straight hair and bangs that skimmed her eyelashes, asked Freddie to introduce his bandmates and to explain how they developed their goofy style. "Are you ever serious?"

"We're very serious about being goofy," Freddie responded, which sent the crowd into stitches.

As the girl interviewed Freddie, the crew set up the next shot for Deedee's number. Around the bottom of the scaffold a five-piece band scrambled to move their instruments into place, and three backup singers gathered around a single microphone.

Deedee stood at the top of the scaffold in a long pink frilly dress. She wore one of the beehive platinum-blond wigs Jobie saw earlier in the dressing room.

The male emcee climbed the scaffold carefully, muttering the whole time under his breath. Jobie smiled, noticing the contrast between his awkwardness and Deedee's confident moves the day before. The producer cued the emcee, and he said, "And now Britain's own answer to American rock and roll. She may start the second American Revolution. Deedee!"

Jobie was unprepared for what came next. She expected some pop confection, similar to the performance of Freddie and the Dreamers. The drummer counted off four beats and the band launched an intro to "Wishin' and Hopin." Like most of Bacharach's songs, it was tricky to sing, staccato in the verse with sustained ballad-like notes in the chorus. Deedee's voice was mesmerizing, strong and husky in the low range and breathy reed-like tones in the upper range. Her breathing throughout seemed natural and unrehearsed, yet perfect. Jobie watched a confident performer who knew that she had a gift. When Jobie closed her eyes, however, she heard a compelling underlying vulnerability. Jobie stood still, holding her guitar to her chest. Deedee's voice was one that would always be instantly recognizable, and one that anybody could fall in love with.

The last strains of the number died away. The studio crowd went wild, both boys and girls jumping up and down and screaming. Deedee bowed low from the waist as the racket from the crowd continued. Her eye caught Jobie's and she smiled, clearly enjoying the crowd's reaction.

Kate came up behind Jobie. "Hey, sorry about snapping at you yesterday. I've just got a lot on my mind, and Deedee wasn't making things any easier."

"Don't think twice."

They watched Deedee climb down the scaffolding. "She's great, isn't she?" Kate said.

"Yes, a natural."

"Oh, don't let appearances fool you. She's been rehearsing with the band and singers all day. She's got them on the edge of mutiny. If it weren't for the calming influence of Marilyn, the other two backup singers and the band would have walked out. I've been concerned that she burned herself out before the show, but she always seems to come through."

Kate rushed away to cue the girl emcee for a game called Rate-A-Record with three members of the audience. "And there you have it, guys and gals," the emcee said. "Our panel gives 'Glad All Over' by the Dave Clark Five a 'ten' because it has a good beat and you can dance to it."

Kate pointed to Jobie, who was so focused on Deedee at the top of the scaffold that she forgot for a moment about her own performance. Technicians wheeled a small moveable stage in front of the camera. She rubbed her hands down the legs of her jeans and took her place on it.

The emcee gave Jobie's intro, "And now, all the way from across the pond, an American girl who is the next big thing in folk music, Jobie Greene."

The studio lights went dark except for one spot directly over her head. The individuals in the audience disappeared into a black mass, and Jobie could barely make out Kate behind the camera, cueing her number. Jobie strummed the first chord. She caught out of the corner of her eye a platinum-blond head at the far edge of the crowd that seemed to glow with a light of its own.

The audience listened politely through "Masters of War," swaying in time with the strumming of Jobie's guitar and sang along enthusiastically with the chorus of "Puff the Magic Dragon." At some point during Jobie's set, Deedee left. When Jobie got back to the dressing room, the only sign of Deedee and the backup singers was a lingering scent of perfume mixed with cigarette smoke.

Jobie collapsed into an overstuffed chair, suddenly let down after the adrenaline rush of performing. She also felt some disappointment that she probably wouldn't see Deedee again. She was scheduled to fly back to New York on Monday. She pulled herself up and opened her guitar case to begin packing. Inside was a note on lavender paper written in a bold, distinctive hand.

Meet us at the Flamingo Club in Soho tonight? Any taxi driver will know where. Marvin Gaye is appearing. We'll be there at ten and I'll save you a chair. D.

Jobie grinned and stuffed the note into her jeans pocket.

Chapter Eighteen

THE TAXI DRIVER PULLED up to the curb in front of the club and waited patiently while Jobie tried to figure out the fare. She gave up and gathered all the coins in her pocket and held them in her outstretched palm while the driver fished out what Jobie trusted was the correct fare plus a tip.

The sign over the doorway read Flamingo Jazz. Beside it was a sign with the logo for Coca-Cola. The club was wedged between a shoe store on the left and a café on the right. Jobie could hear a heavy R & B beat coming from inside. As she got closer to the club door, she could make out the sweet tenor of Marvin Gaye's voice. She stood in the doorway, letting her eyes get used to the dim interior.

Deedee and her crew were sitting directly in front of the small stage. Jobie recognized Kate and Deedee's backup singers, Marilyn, Betty, and Peggy. As good as her word, Deedee had kept a vacant chair for Jobie on her right and was watching for her. As soon as the last note died and the enthusiastic applause started, she stood and motioned Jobie over.

Deedee pulled Jobie's chair close to hers and put her arm on the back. In the low light, Jobie stole a sideways glance at Deedee as she joked with her friends around the table. Without her wig and stage makeup, she looked younger, confirming Jobie's guess that she was about her age. After just two days in London, Jobie was already beginning to be able to differentiate among the sounds of people's accents: the Liverpool sing-song of the Beatles always on the edge of sarcasm; the rounded vowels of Manchester natives like Freddy and the Dreamers; and the "posh" sounds of upper-middle-class Londoners. She guessed that Deedee fit in the last category.

"You know that bar service doesn't work the same way here as in America, right?" Deedee asked. "You have to go up and order for yourself. Here, I'll go with you."

The two women got their beers, and as they were returning to the table, Marvin Gaye called out, "Ladies and gentlemen, tonight we have a treat. In the audience is a young lady whose first album has just hit the record stores, and it's selling like, well, like fish and chips. She didn't know I was going to do this, but I'm inviting her to come up for a duet on one of the tracks on that album, 'Mockingbird.' Welcome Deedee!"

The crowd broke into loud applause as all eyes in the club turned toward the two women standing with beers in their hands, halfway between the bar and their table. Deedee handed her beer to Jobie and strode to the small stage.

With only the twang of the funky lead electric guitar accompanying them, Deedee and Marvin Gaye rocked through the popular R & B song. Deedee's proper accent was replaced by authentic American phrasing. Marvin Gaye's three-octave range and Deedee's strong chest voice complimented each other perfectly. She seemed completely at ease and not intimidated by this particularly American music style.

The crowd rose to their feet with their hands in the air, demanding verse after verse, and finally, running out of words, Deedee and Marvin were ad-libbing and scat singing in perfect harmony with each other. Deedee signaled the guitarist that she was done, and the final chord sounded. The room erupted as she hugged Marvin Gaye and ran off the stage back to their table.

"That was amazing," Jobie shouted in her ear over the noise. "Where did you learn to sing R & B?"

"I've been to America, to Nashville and to Detroit. I'm working with Kate right now to put on an entire Motown-sound show for *Thank Your Lucky Stars.*

"You sounded as though you've been singing it your whole life. And to stand toe to toe with Marvin Gaye...you're fearless."

"He makes it seem easy."

They were interrupted by Kate, shouting across the table to get Deedee's attention. "We should go, before they ask you to sing again. You don't want to cheapen the merchandise by giving too much away."

Deedee smiled at Jobie. "I don't think she's even aware when she treats me like a can of soup. I suppose she's right, though. What are you doing tomorrow night? We're having a gang over for spaghetti if you can come." She handed Jobie a piece of the same lavender paper as the note in her guitar case. On the note, she had printed an address on Westbourne Terrace and "8:00."

Jobie took the paper. "You were so sure I would show up tonight?"

"I was pretty confident you would." She smiled as she helped Jobie on with her jacket.

"Oh, you were, were you?" Jobie felt a tickle of pleasure that she would get to spend more time with Deedee before going back to the US.

***

Westbourne Terrace was a wide boulevard near Hyde Park, lined on both sides with white Regency-style houses connected by common walls. From the street in the dark the houses looked imposing, with elegant columns in front, wrought iron fences next to the sidewalks, and second-story balconies. Jobie double-checked the address written on Deedee's note and climbed the six steps from the sidewalk to the double entry doors.

Getting closer, she saw what passed for elegance from the street faded a bit up close. She saw that the doors of the building were slightly ajar. She could hear the loud, steady pulse of a bass guitar. She didn't bother ringing the bell, sure that no one would hear it. She tentatively pushed the door open wider and slid sideways into a long, narrow hallway. Down the hallway at the end was another open door from which the music was coming. The bass was so loud in the hallway that she didn't just hear it but felt it as a pulsing of her insides. The music was joined by buzzing conversation and laughter.

She walked down the hallway and peeked inside the open door. The apartment was tiny and packed with people. Two studio-sized speakers occupied a full quarter of the floor space of the one room that appeared to serve as a combination sitting room, bedroom, and kitchen. Against one wall, a cabinet held what Jobie assumed was a pull-down Murphy bed.

The big speakers were blasting "Dancing in the Street," a tune from the Motown group Martha and the Vandellas. Jobie laughed out loud when she saw that the group's lead singer, Martha Reeves herself, was sitting on the floor with her legs tucked under her. Beyond French doors that were propped open, a small patio held the overflow of the crowd.

Deedee was standing over the stove in the corner of the room that served as a kitchen, stirring something in an enormous pot. She looked up when Jobie came in the door and waved her over with the wooden spoon in her hand.

"You found me!"

"I told the taxi driver to just follow the noise," Jobie said. "You must have very tolerant neighbors."

"They're all here, so no worries." She leaned past Jobie and opened a tiny refrigerator. "Take a beer and introduce yourself around while I get this spaghetti served up. Kate's here, and Marilyn." Deedee stood on tiptoe and looked over the crowd. "Maybe out on the patio."

Jobie was in no hurry to find Kate. She felt from their first meeting in the *Thank Your Lucky Stars* studio that Kate had more than just a professional interest in Deedee. The producer had been nice enough the next night at the show, but Jobie felt she was threatened by Deedee's friendliness toward Jobie.

Jobie sipped her beer and circulated around the edges of the crowd, joining conversations where she found an opening. Most of the people she met were in the music business—backup musicians, production assistants, or junior talent agents. They recognized her from her appearance on *TYLS* and expressed polite interest in American folk music, but not much familiarity with the genre.

A gong sounded over the booming music, a signal that the food was ready. Deedee had laid out a buffet with huge bowls of spaghetti, red sauce, crusty garlic bread, green salad, and bottles of red wine. Everyone queued up to fill their plates while Deedee stood with her hands on her hips encouraging each person to take more.

Jobie found a spot to sit cross-legged on the floor. She gingerly tested to find a safe balancing spot on her knees for her plate of spaghetti and on the floor for her full glass of red wine.

As she was getting settled, Marilyn walked up with her plate and wineglass. "Mind if I join you?"

"Please." Jobie scooted over to make more room. As Marilyn sat down beside her, Jobie admired the scarlet embroidered dashiki that she wore over black slacks. The color and style complimented her dark skin and neat Afro. "You're American, too, right?"

"Yes, Baltimore. And you?"

"Originally from near Chattanooga, Tennessee, and now New York. How did you get to London?"

Marilyn inched closer to Jobie to be heard over the booming speakers. "I came across, I thought just for a few weeks, and I've been here a year so far. Deedee heard me singing in an East End club. She came up after my set. She was just getting started as a solo act then. She asked me if I did session work." Marilyn smiled at the memory. "I was so green, I asked her what that meant. She was starting recording her first album, and she thought my voice in backup would work for the sound she had in mind. I've been singing with her ever since."

"What about your own solo career?"

"I'm young. There's always time for that. I'm learning so much from Deedee that I figure it's worth the investment."

"Deedee's young, too. What are you learning from her?"

"She knows exactly the sound she's looking for. She won't compromise. I've seen her pull us all into a stairwell or a loo if she likes the acoustics better than in the studio. Sometimes I think she likes producing the records better than singing on them. She basically produces her own records, but in this business, a woman has to pretend to give someone else the credit for that. Deedee thinks that to be a success, she has to pretend to be just a singer."

"Is that true?"

"Seems to be working for her." Jobie remembered what Kate said at the *Thank Your Lucky Stars* show, about Deedee paying a high price for her perfectionism.

"What about Kate? She seems to be succeeding as a TV producer. Most of them are men."

"Yes, Kate is exceptional." Marilyn nodded toward Kate, who was the last one in the buffet line. She stood holding her empty plate, leaning over the table in an intense conversation with Deedee. Kate appeared to be doing most of the talking with Deedee nodding or shaking her head in response.

"We live in the flat just above, Kate and I." Marilyn gestured toward the ceiling with her wineglass.

"She seems to be a good friend to Deedee. Very protective."

Marilyn kept her eyes on her spaghetti. "Yes, they're very close." She drained her wine, rose from her spot on the floor, and gestured toward Jobie's glass. "More?"

"Not yet, thanks."

Jobie watched Deedee take off her sauce-stained apron and cross the room to the phonograph turntable. Another Martha and the Vandellas tune, "Heatwave," blasted out of the speakers. The song was a number-one hit in the US the year before, but unreleased in the UK.

Deedee pulled Martha close and the two of them began singing along with the record, Martha taking the lead with Deedee singing backup. Marilyn and another singer whom Jobie hadn't met joined them on the makeshift stage. Everyone in the room rose to their feet, and those on the patio crowded inside, all clapping their hands to the infectious beat and dancing as much as the tight quarters would allow. Jobie saw the look on Deedee's face—one of pure unselfconscious elation—as the song ended, and she embraced Martha and urged the crowd's applause for her. She seemed completely at ease taking a back seat to Martha.

"More, more!" the partiers demanded, but Deedee shook her head, filled her own plate, navigated through the crowd, and settled on the floor next to Jobie. Again, as when she watched her climb down the scaffold in the TV studio, Jobie noticed Deedee's physical grace.

People seemed to be content letting the blasting speakers take a rest while they ate their spaghetti. The low buzz of conversations replaced the music.

Jobie held her wineglass up for a mock salute to Deedee. "Is there no end to your talents? This spaghetti sauce is almost as good as your Motown sound."

"They're both just for fun." She deflected the conversation away from herself. "What are your plans, now that the TV show is done?"

"I go back to New York tomorrow."

"Oh, so soon? In and out that quickly?" Deedee sipped her wine.

"Yes, this was more an experiment by the record label than a real tour or anything. I suppose some marketing person will follow up by trying to make a distribution deal for my music here in the UK. I don't get involved with the business side at all."

"Some would say I get involved too much in it." Deedee gestured with her wineglass across the room toward Kate. "My friend the TV producer over there thinks I need a full-time manager. I suppose the time is going to come when I do."

"Marilyn was telling me how you basically produce your own records."

"Yes, that's one thing I'll never give up. I'm too much of a perfectionist, I suppose. It's the part of the process that I can truly say I enjoy. I could see letting Kate take care of the rest of it, but I would feel a big responsibility. I'd be taking her away from her successful TV career to work with me full time."

Jobie again wanted to ask Deedee about her personal relationship with Kate, but she hesitated, and the moment passed.

"Hey, why are we wasting time talking business? You're going back to the US. I'd hoped to get to know you better."

Jobie felt a rush of pleasure. "I'd like that."

Deedee and Jobie flinched in unison as the giant speakers boomed to life with the opening chord of the intro to another Motown hit. Marilyn ran over and pulled Deedee to her feet for another impromptu performance.

Chapter Nineteen

DAMN! JOBIE GRABBED HER bedside alarm clock and shook it, which made no sense. It wasn't the clock's fault that she had forgotten to turn on the alarm. She struggled to free her legs from the tangled sheets. Thankfully, she had packed her suitcase and laid out the day's clothes at the foot of the bed the night before. She anticipated that in the best case, it would be a race to catch the train for a five-hour trip to Newport, Rhode Island, for her appearance at the Newport Folk Festival. Now she had made it more of a sprint.

She wiggled into her jeans, pulled on a linen blouse, and buckled her leather sandals. *Time for coffee? Buy it on the way somewhere.*

The bedside phone jangled. *Damn again. Deedee.* The phone calls started as soon as Jobie landed back in the States from London, at first once a week or so, then becoming an almost daily part of Jobie's morning routine over the past several weeks. Deedee called at seven in the morning in New York and noon in London. She usually slept late after a performance or a recording session. The first few times Jobie complained about the early hour, but Deedee argued that between their two schedules and the time zone differences, this was the best option. Jobie eventually came to accept the early calls.

She grabbed the phone. "Hello, Deedee. I don't have time to talk this morning. I've made myself late leaving for Newport." Jobie tucked the phone between her ear and shoulder and stretched the cord till she could barely reach the handle of her guitar case. She pulled it over to the bed and opened it, taking a quick inventory of the guitar, spare strings, picks, capos, and a notebook.

Deedee was undeterred. "Oh, no. Well, just quickly, exciting news. I just found out today. As soon as we're done with the new album, I'm going to Cape Town, South Africa for two concerts. Kate's coming with me to produce the whole thing. Marilyn and the girls will be along to sing backup. I know you can't talk now, but just think about this. Go with us. Open for me."

"Deedee, you know I can't go into South Africa. They're not going to let a mixed-race American protest singer in. Most of my songs are about resisting authority, stopping wars, and breaking chains. That wouldn't go over well with the powers that be in South Africa, I'm sure. I'm surprised you're willing to go."

"Oh, I've got that covered. My contract says I'll play only to integrated audiences."

"How did you pull that off?"

"Kate worked with the record label attorneys and the British Consulate in Cape Town."

"Still, you and Kate are white. I'd be a different matter, and so will Marilyn, if she's going. And what makes you think black South Africans can even afford tickets to your concerts?"

Deedee paused. "Then I'll give the tickets away. Just keep an open mind. Think about it. You have to go now, I know. We can talk later. Have fun at the festival."

"Goodbye, Deedee." Jobie ran a comb through her hair, threw on a fringed suede jacket, grabbed her guitar and suitcase, and ran out her front door to hail a cab to the station.

***

Jobie stood at the bottom of the steps leading up to the stage. The fine mist that persisted all week at the Newport Folk Festival had turned the grass, beaten down by the wanderings of a hundred thousand people, into mud. Jobie looked down at her feet in Mexican sandals with soles made from old tires. They would have been perfect for a dry, warm August night in Newport, but the cloud cover all day dropped the temperature down to the sixties.

The weather hadn't driven away this crowd who came on the last night to see Bob Dylan, and incidentally any other acts who were set to appear. She counted herself one of the incidental other acts. The master of ceremonies for the evening, one of the male members of a popular folk trio, announced her name. Jobie clutched her guitar in one sweaty hand and gripped the handrail with the other to climb the stairs.

On stage, she adjusted the microphone and looked out over the upturned faces of what seemed to her the biggest audience ever on earth, seated on wooden folding chairs that stretched a quarter of a mile back to circus tents with restrooms and medic stations. Below the stage, in the pit, Jobie caught a glimpse of a tall woman with platinum-blond hair, the same color as one of Deedee's wigs. For a moment, Jobie had the irrational thought that the woman was Deedee, but her hair was long and straight with bangs, not the teased beehive Deedee wore.

The sound system screeched. She adjusted the mic again, strummed a chord, and tightened a string. She sang two Tennessee songs, "Down in the Valley" and "Ain't Gonna Study War No More," then hustled off the stage in the middle of polite applause. She felt acutely aware that the crowd was restless for Dylan's appearance. Though there were no printed programs, the crowd sensed that Dylan was up soon. Sounds of muted rustling and shuffling rose from the audience as the master of ceremonies came back to the mic. Jobie found a place to stand in the pit, next to the woman with platinum hair. Behind the emcee on the stage, roadies rushed to push out a drum set, an organ, and several large amplifiers.

The emcee stepped to the mic. "Down through time, people, and I suppose all living beings for that matter, have sung songs when we felt there were things that needed to be said. This man who's coming up next sings what a whole generation needs to have said. He's more than a singer. He's a prophet and a hero. Ladies and gentlemen, welcome Bob Dylan."

The crowd erupted as with one voice when Dylan climbed the steps, followed by four other musicians, two carrying electric guitars. Dylan strapped on his Fender Stratocaster and launched into an electrified version of "Maggie's Farm." The crowd gasped in unison, and then began jeering and yelling sounds of dismay and betrayal, loud enough to drown out the singer and his band.

Standing in the pit in front of the stage, Jobie was close enough to see the shaken look on Dylan's face, but he carried on with the set. When he finished the first song, he stepped away from the microphone and signaled the band for the intro to his newest recording, "Like a Rolling Stone." The crowd noise continued.

The hairs stood up on the back of Jobie's neck. She suspected she was witness to history, the beginning of Dylan's evolution from acoustic folk to electrified pop singer.

The blond woman next to her spoke. "Wow!" She leaned toward Jobie to be heard over the noise. "We'll tell our grandchildren we were here for this."

Hearing her voice, Jobie recognized her with a shock. She was the female member of the trio The Travelers, the same group as the emcee. Jobie hadn't placed her without the presence of the bookends of her two trio-mates. The Travelers were the country's most commercially successful folk act.

"I'm Clair." The woman stuck out her hand, and Jobie transferred her guitar to her left hand so she could acknowledge the greeting.

"I'm Jobie. I'm a big fan of yours."

Clair smiled her thanks. "I enjoyed your set." She gestured toward the stage. "After his set, do you want to find some place where we can talk? I suspect you and I may have lots in common, being women in this business at this time in history."

"I'd like that."

Dylan played one more electrified song, then replaced his Stratocaster with an acoustic guitar for two unaccompanied numbers. The crowd's mood turned a little more positive, but the applause was subdued, and Dylan walked off stage without acknowledging the applause or offering an encore.

Jobie and Clair stood speechless, watching Dylan disappear around the corner of the stage. "Well," Clair said. "We'll read about this in the trades, no doubt. Maybe they'll be able to get behind what he has in mind."

"I asked him once, in the Gaslight, about his inspiration for the lyrics to his songs. He told me he just writes what people want to hear. He may have misjudged this crowd. They clearly didn't want to hear a rock-and-roll Dylan."

"Maybe he's just way ahead of us all." Clair took Jobie's elbow and steered her toward a line of white vans. "We can take the tram to where I'm staying, if you like. They've given us rooms in the Vanderbilts' summer cottage. It's a grand old mansion with a terrace that overlooks the harbor. Very pleasant."

Clair picked a path for them through the fans milling around, hoping for a close encounter with their idols. The two women signed a few autographs, and then found a van with its motor running. Clair stuck her head in to ask the driver, "Can you drive us to The Breakers?"

"Sure thing." The driver headed the van for the main road, maneuvering carefully around groups of fans and musicians loading equipment.

They drove south down the peninsula that jutted into Newport Harbor. To their right, the sun was beginning to set, inflaming low-hanging clouds with oranges and yellows. They rode in silence, Clair seeming preoccupied with her own thoughts, and Jobie was reluctant to interrupt her.

Jobie sneaked occasional glances at Clair's profile against the van window. A slight hump in her nose marred the perfection of her features, making her looks even more interesting to Jobie. Her silver hair, parted in the middle, hung perfectly straight to her shoulders. She had a habit of tossing her head to punctuate a point or emphasize a musical phrase. When she did, her hair rustled like silk fringe.

The van rounded the tip of the peninsula and headed north along the water for a few more minutes, finally turning into a circular gravel drive in front of an enormous Renaissance-style palazzo built from honey-colored stone.

Jobie looked up at the façade of the three-story mansion. "I thought you said this was a summer cottage. I pictured something a little more rustic and modest."

"I know. Summer cottage is what the Vanderbilts called it. Whether they were being serious or ironic has been lost to history. Wait till you see the inside. The youngest Vanderbilt daughter donated the estate years ago to the Preservation Society, furnishings and all, so you have the feeling of being in a time warp, back to the turn of the century. The festival organizers gave the two guys and me rooms in the family quarters, so we're not on the visitor's tour during the days. Let's go out on the terrace, and I'll see if I can find us something to drink."

Clair led Jobie through the opulent formal sitting room and out French doors onto the terrace. The back of the mansion faced east, and the sun was already setting behind the red tile roof of the house. "We can look east over the water, or we can turn our chairs west and catch the last rays of the sunset over the top of the roof. What's your pleasure?"

Jobie gazed out across the perfectly groomed back lawn that led down to a narrow strip of sand, and beyond that, the Atlantic. The water, in the daytime clear blue, had already darkened to indigo, except for glittering whitecaps that broke placidly on the shore. "Water view," Jobie said.

"Good choice." Clair disappeared into the house and came back with a bottle of white wine in one hand and two stemmed glasses in the other. "I hope white's okay." She held the label forward with a flourish for Jobie to inspect, mimicking a sommelier in a fine restaurant.

Clair moved a chair next to Jobie's, close enough that the arms touched. She filled two glasses with wine, settled back in her chair and blew out a long breath. "I don't know about you, but I'm glad to see this week done. Cheers!" She held her wine up to Jobie's for a toast, and their glasses rang with the clear tone of crystal.

They sipped their wine in silence for a time, watching a flock of seagulls land on the lawn and peck in the grass until one, as if reacting to some signal, took flight, drawing the rest with him out to sea.

Jobie asked, "You haven't enjoyed the festival this year?"

"Oh, don't mind me. It's just that Mel and Don and I have done nothing but squabble the whole time about what to sing, Mel wanted to do our tried and true book, and Don wanted more of the new stuff. We've even argued about what I'd wear on stage. Can you imagine?"

Jobie was surprised by Clair's talk of discord in the trio. She admitted to herself that, like the public, she took the group's close vocal harmony on stage for an indication that they got along in private. "It must be a challenge sometimes to be in synch with two other entertainers, but why would they think they could have an opinion about what you wear?"

"Oh, it's just general unease about our place in the business right now. You don't look old enough to have much experience on where we've been since 1960. You saw what happened with Dylan today. None of us knows the future of our music between the so-called British Invasion and the Motown sound." Clair filled Jobie's glass and her own.

"If you look at the charts, the songs are all the Beatles, the Stones, Petula Clark, the Temptations. It's either British pop or Motown R & B, not folk. The only place The Travelers are still doing well is on our college tours. Even there we don't always play to full houses. Our album sales are still okay, but who knows for how long? My manager wants me to go solo with a pop album."

Clair tossed her head, making her silvery hair shimmer in the moonlight. "Let's change the subject. I didn't invite you for a drink so I could complain about the music business, but I have to admit it's nice to have someone to talk to. That's the end of my rant." Clair lightly patted Jobie's hand, and the touch turned into a light caress. "Tell me about you. Do you live in New York?"

Jobie nodded. "On Washington Square."

"Nice."

"Yes, and way beyond my means. I moved north after high school and slept on people's couches for a year. Once my break came, and I signed with the record label, I splurged on the apartment. Optimistic."

"Seems to be working for you. Tell me about your break."

"Totally out of the blue. A girl singer at the Gaslight came down with the flu, throwing up in the ladies' room. I borrowed her guitar and sang a half-hour set. It happened so fast I didn't have time to be nervous. There was an A and R guy there from Columbia."

"But you're with Vanguard, right? Why did you decide to sign with them?"

"I had to choose between Vanguard and Columbia. It was a hard choice, but I guess I'm okay with the one I made." Jobie sipped her wine and watched the seagulls fly out to sea then circle back toward land again. "I chose for such a superficial reason. Columbia's halls are lined with gold records and Vanguard's walls are bare. I thought that meant that Columbia would be all about money and Vanguard all about music, but I've learned that every record company is in the business more or less to make a profit. I think Vanguard is better about letting me play mostly small venues, like coffeehouses, and not so insistent that I tour."

The thought of tours took her mind back to London, then to Deedee and their discussion about the trip to South Africa. She rested her head against the back of the chair and closed her eyes, listening to the steady wash of small waves against the sandy spit of beach beyond the lawn. Clair was close enough that Jobie could smell the subtle drift of a floral perfume, and underneath that a clean scent of soap.

"Do you live alone?" Clair's tone was neutral, but the question held more intimacy because it was asked almost in a whisper.

Jobie opened her eyes and looked at Clair's smiling face, only barely visible in the gathering gloom. "Yes."

Clair nodded, and her silvery hair ruffled in a slight breeze and reflected the moonlight.

Jobie reached a hand toward Clair's hair and hesitated. "May I?" Clair nodded again, and Jobie ran her fingers through Clair's hair. "I've wondered if your hair could possibly feel the way it looks. It does."

Clair smiled, leaned toward Jobie, and placed a kiss lightly on her mouth. Her lips were cool and dry on Jobie's, and the kiss felt as chaste as one you might give a sister. "And I've wanted to know how your lips felt all evening. Turnabout is fair play."

Jobie nodded, but Clair made no move to kiss her again. "You live alone, but I'm guessing you're involved."

Jobie puzzled over how to respond. Would she call a weekend meeting and a month of phone calls with Deedee "involved"?

"I think I may be." Jobie surprised herself by responding that way. "Figures."

The French doors behind them opened and Clair's two trio partners, Mel and Don, came through. "Here you are," the taller one said. "We wondered where you'd got off to."

Clair introduced Jobie to Mel and Don and rose to go into the kitchen for another bottle of wine and glasses while the men pulled up chairs to create front row seats for watching the gathering dark over the water.

"Hope we're not interrupting anything," Don said. "We're too used to pushing into each other's business, I suppose."

"No, we were just talking about Dylan's performance tonight and where the business is going."

"Don't listen to Clair and Mel on that subject," Don said. "They'll make you think the sky is falling. We've all had a great run so far. We'll always find our audience, as long as we want to carry on with this mad rat race."

Clair came back with the wine, and Don continued. "We'll do fine as long as we can keep Clair looking sexy and Mel writing great songs."

"So, what does that make you—" "What about you—" Mel and Clair shot back over each other.

"I'm the only one who can play a decent guitar and sing harmony." He ducked as Clair threw the wine cork at him. "I think we've been incredibly lucky, no matter how much longer our popularity lasts. Who else gets to stay for free in a spread like this? Where did they put you?" he asked Jobie.

"North of here, inland. It's called the Bell House. Much more modest."

"And less like staying in a museum," Mel said. "I'll trade with you."

The four of them finished the second bottle of wine, and Jobie declined when Clair offered to open another bottle. "I need to find my way to Bell House. I'm going back to New York tomorrow and playing at Café Wha? tomorrow night. As Don would advise, I need my beauty rest to try and keep my audience."

Don pitched Clair his car keys. "It's parked in the drive out front."

The engine of Don's car, a red Jaguar sedan, started with a throaty roar. Clair expertly navigated the car through the deserted streets of the peninsula. Pulling up in front of Jobie's place, Clair shut off the engine and turned toward Jobie. "I believe we live within a few blocks of each other in the city. Would you like to get together for dinner some night?"

This time it was Jobie who leaned across the console to Clair. The kiss began tentatively but deepened as Jobie felt Clair overcome surprise and return the pressure of her lips. They squirmed to get closer together, thwarted by the console, and Jobie pulled Clair across it into her lap. She held the kiss with her hand at the back of Clair's head, feeling the silken flow of her hair down her forearm. Clair pulled back to catch her breath and looked at Jobie.

"Before we get carried away, what about your being involved?"

"That's a long story. Well, not really long, but maybe unclear is a better word. I met someone in London a few weeks ago. I was there just for a weekend. A TV appearance."

"Okay." Clair rested her back against the dashboard and waited for Jobie to go on.

Jobie smoothed the cowlick at her hairline. "I think I have feelings for her, but I couldn't really after just meeting her and with nothing having happened between us. Could I? And I suspect she may be involved with someone else."

Clair climbed back over the console to the driver's side. She had kicked off her pumps when Jobie began kissing her. Before responding, she bent to retrieve them. "How old are you, Jobie?"

"Twenty-two." She tossed off the response, careful to keep her tone matter-of-fact. "Not that much younger than you, I think."

Clair smiled and nodded her head. "Give yourself some time to find out what your feelings are for her. The dinner invitation still stands." She opened the glove compartment and fished around until she found a pen and a scrap of paper. "Here's my phone number."

Jobie stood on the edge of the lawn and watched the taillights of the Jaguar disappear as Clair turned the corner, headed back toward The Breakers.

Chapter Twenty

SUNDAY MORNINGS IN WASHINGTON Square were Jobie's favorite times in New York. Growing up in Tennessee, she dreamed of coming to the big city with the sureness of a premonition. She stepped out of the door of her brownstone apartment and paused at the top of the steps to take in the view of the park across the street, beyond the arch where Fifth Avenue dead-ended at the square. She carried her sketchbook and charcoals, planning to find a sunny bench across from the fountain where she could sit and draw. These days, it was rare that she could devote time to her passion for drawing and painting. Since signing with the record label, she felt duty-bound to spend all her free time practicing or preparing for appearances.

She had expected a call this morning from Deedee, since she hadn't heard from her the day before. Jobie could picture her recording into the early morning to get every line and every measure perfect. During their last call, she said that the album would be wrapping up any day.

High-pitched squeals of children playing in the fountain bounced off the encircling buildings in the heavy autumn air and drew her attention back to the park. Two elderly men were hunched over their chessboard with the intensity of opposing generals planning a real war. A young man strummed an acoustic guitar and blew on a harmonica in a neck holder, his guitar case open in front of him to encourage donations.

Jobie remembered busking the same way in the park during the first year she came to New York. If she were honest, she'd have to admit that she enjoyed music more back then. She skipped down the steps, jaywalked across the street, quiet at this time of the morning, and paused to drop a dollar bill into the young man's mostly empty case. The smile he gave her was so beautiful that tears sprang up behind her eyes. She nodded to him and hurried east past the park toward Veniero's Bakery, a fixture in the East Village since the nineteenth century and her favorite place for a morning coffee and pastry.

The tiny brass bell over the door tinkled as she entered the shop that had changed little in seven decades. The marble floors, etched glass, and hand-stamped tin ceiling were original from when Antonio

Veniero first began selling his grandmother's old country recipe biscotti in 1894.

"Ah, *bella cantante*." Frank, Antonio's great-grandson, greeted her from behind the lighted glass case of rainbow-colored confections. "Your usual today?"

"Yes, Frank, but I'll take it to go. The weather's too beautiful to sit inside this morning."

She headed back across Second Avenue and toward the park, looking for a vacant bench that offered a view of the fountain, the arch, and Fifth Avenue north to the Empire State Building. Out of habit, she glanced across the street toward her apartment building and saw someone sitting on the steps leading up to her front door. She could hardly believe her eyes. It was Deedee. They met in the middle of the street. Jobie swept Deedee up and twirled her around. She fumbled with her pastries, coffee, sketchbook, and key, and drew Deedee up the steps and inside the front door of her apartment.

"How did you get here? Why didn't you tell me you were coming? What if I had been gone?"

"Then I would have sat out there on your front stoop until you came home. It's a spur-of-the-moment trip. I'm desperate for the right tune to finish the album, and Burt Bacharach is my last hope. I'm meeting him tomorrow morning at the Brill Building. Want to come?"

"Of course, I'd love to, but I have a meeting at Vanguard." Jobie pulled Deedee down on the sofa.

"Cancel it and come with me."

"Deedee, you can't just show up and expect me to drop everything."

"I wanted to surprise you. I thought you'd be glad to see me."

"Of course, I'm glad to see you. I love it that you came all this way to see me, at least partly to see me." She noticed that she was still clutching the bag of pastries from Veniero's. "Are you hungry? Your internal clock must say it's teatime. I'll make us some tea and you can share my pastries. I guarantee they're delicious."

She went to put on the kettle in her small kitchen.

Deedee picked up the sketchbook from the coffee table where Jobie had left it. "May I?" She thumbed slowly through Jobie's sketches of Village life and portraits of characters she saw on the streets. Deedee raised her eyebrows. "These are wonderful. Especially the portraits. Why didn't you tell me you're an artist? I have so much respect and even envy of anyone who can do this."

"It's a hobby. I don't spend as much time on it as I'd like."

Deedee patted the couch cushion next to her. "Forget the tea for a while. Come over here and sit with me, Jobie. I've traveled all the way across the Atlantic to see you."

Jobie set the kettle down. "I have to ask you a question first."

"What?"

"When I was in London and I saw you and Kate together, I thought maybe that the two of you might be involved. Marilyn hinted as much."

Deedee sat forward with her elbows on her knees. "Please, come over here and sit down so I can talk to you."

Jobie crossed the room and sat on the sofa.

"You're right. Kate and I are very close. She's always been my biggest fan. She encouraged me to go solo when I was too afraid to leave the group I was singing with. I wouldn't have had the nerve to go out on my own without her encouragement. She and I share a love of R & B music and the Motown sound. I told you she's going to work with me to produce a special Motown show on *TYLS*. Now she's trying to convince me that she should be my manager. I think she's right, but I would feel a big responsibility if she left her TV career to be with me full time."

Jobie nodded. "You told me about that, but I'm not talking about your professional relationship." Jobie stood and looked out the windows toward the park. She stuffed her fists in her jeans pockets. "I'm not asking about that." She blew out a breath in frustration. "This is so hard. I have no right to quiz you about it."

"Ask me whatever you want."

"Have you been to bed with her?"

"Yes, but that's in the past."

"What happened?"

"I wouldn't say anything happened. She just wanted more from the relationship than I was prepared to give. More of a commitment to being exclusive, I mean." Deedee laughed. "That doesn't put me in a very good light, does it?"

Deedee went on, but Jobie could hear a note of impatience in her voice. "Kate and I agreed our friendship and her helping me build a career was more important than the other." Deedee took hold of Jobie's arm and drew her back down beside her on the sofa. "Do we have to waste time talking about this? I'm here right now, with you. Can't we just enjoy that?"

Jobie faced a choice. She could do as Deedee said and enjoy the fact that she was here in New York without her frilly yellow dress, platinum beehive wig, and backup singers, sitting in Jobie's living room just as Jobie dreamed she someday would be, or she could risk spoiling the moment by worrying about a future. She took Deedee in her arms and kissed her with passion stored up over the weeks since England.

Deedee pulled back, laughing, "Now this is the reception I was looking for. Slow down a little and let me look at you up close. I confess I'm nearsighted and too vain to wear glasses. I thought you couldn't be as lovely as I'd remembered, but you are." Deedee smoothed the cowlick on Jobie's forehead and took her face in her hands. She drew her in for a slower, deeper kiss.

Jobie pressed Deedee down on the sofa, caressing her face, neck, and shoulders. "You're really here."

Deedee laughed, and when Jobie began to massage her breasts, the laugh turned into a moan of surprised pleasure. Jobie pulled Deedee's sweater over her head and unfastened her bra, stripping off her own sweatshirt as well.

Jobie sat back on her heels and they both stopped motionless for a moment, smiling into each other's eyes, then fumbled to pull off the rest of their constraining clothes and paused again as four hands covered four bare breasts. Jobie bent to Deedee and made slow love to her, watching and listening for cues in the vibrations of her body and memorizing the tempos of her passion until she trembled with a shuddering climax. Jobie lay down beside her and traced her profile with the tip of her index finger over and over, slowly from her forehead, over her nose, across her lips and chin to her throat. Sounds of the children playing in the park across the street drifted in the window. Deedee lay so still that Jobie thought she must have fallen asleep until Deedee reached up to take her hand and kiss each fingertip.

"Is that your bedroom?" She motioned across the room to a door.

"Yes. Do you want a nap? You must be worn out from your overnight plane trip."

Deedee smiled. "No." She led Jobie by the hand into the bedroom, sat on the side of the bed, and pulled Jobie down to sit astride her thighs. "I've pictured being with you this way ever since that first day we met in the television studio. Put your arms around my shoulders."

Jobie felt Deedee's hand enfold her most sensitive spot and begin a gentle caressing rhythm as she held their naked breasts against each other and kissed her deeply. Jobie's hips involuntarily moved in time with the rhythmic, relentless stroking, and she heard her own breaths become shallow gasps.

Deedee pulled away from the kiss with a question in her eyes.

"Yes, yes. Go inside me." Her voice was a hoarse croak. The tempo quickened and Jobie's pelvis arched to press into Deedee's hand. The sensations built to a crescendo and blocked out everything, the room, the bed, even Deedee so that all of Jobie's awareness centered on the pleasure of her orgasm. She fell against Deedee, half whimpering and half laughing.

Deedee lowered the two of them to lie side by side on the bed. "Are you okay?" She gently stroked Jobie's face. "What can I get you, some water?"

"Just sing to me. I want to hear you sing." She drifted off to sleep with Deedee's beautiful, special voice in her ears.

Chapter Twenty-one

JOBIE CAME OFTEN TO L's on MacDougal Street. It was one of the few Greenwich Village bars catering to lesbians that wasn't owned by the Mafia. There was no beefy bouncer at the front door blocking Deedee and Jobie's entrance, and no cover charge. The bathrooms were clean, and while men were not expressly prohibited, they were discouraged. The atmosphere inside was more like that of a club meeting of professional women, and the crowd tended to be androgynous rather than divided into butches and femmes.

Deedee found a small table for them, and as Jobie went to the bar for a gin for Deedee and a beer for herself, she noticed the buzz in the club grow louder. Either Deedee or she, or both of them, had been recognized.

A jukebox in the corner played mellow music as a few couples swayed together on the tiny dance floor, each twosome in their own small circle. Jobie stood at the bar waiting for their drinks and watched women whisper behind their hands and gesture toward the table where Deedee sat smiling at her. Jobie wound her way between the dancing couples back to the table. Deedee jumped up and pulled out Jobie's chair, her hand brushing lightly across Jobie's breast, as though by accident, as she sat down. Jobie smiled.

She set their drinks on the table. "I don't know how you drink gin straight without ice."

"'On-the-rocks' is strictly an American invention. The ice melts and dilutes the booze."

"Humph." Jobie sniffed.

The music switched to one of the up-tempo pop songs from Deedee's first album. A woman leaning against the jukebox smiled at Deedee and held up her beer bottle in a salute. Deedee returned the woman's smile and raised her glass.

Jobie tensed. What if the fan read Deedee's gesture as an invitation to approach them? She turned her chair so that her back was to the jukebox. "You've been made, as they say on the cop shows."

"How do you know it's me and not you?"

"They might recognize me, but I'm old hat in L's. You're the new face. Do you want to leave?"

"No. They'll get used to me soon enough. It's nice, really. Besides, if I'm going to be a success, I've got to get better known in the US. It's a good sign that I'm being recognized." Deedee shot another quick glance toward the fan at the jukebox.

"Do you have to flirt? What if she comes over?"

"Then we'll both be gracious and give her an autograph or whatever. She's cute."

Jobie opened her mouth to ask her if she was deliberately leading the woman on but stopped herself and instead changed the subject. "I'm sorry things didn't work out today with Burt Bacharach. He seems especially anxious to have you record one of his songs."

"Thank you for going with me."

"The Vanguard A and R guy was not happy that I cancelled at the last minute, but I guess he'll get over it."

At the Brill Building on Broadway, Deedee and Bacharach had spent the whole day in a rehearsal room with Jobie sitting silent in a corner. Bacharach played song after song on an ancient, out-of-tune upright piano, and Deedee sight-read from handwritten sheet music. Bacharach sometimes joined in with his distinctive talk/sing style.

Jobie fought the urge to applaud after every song. She listened carefully to catch the essence of what Deedee was looking for in this final song to finish off her second album. Jobie could have chosen any one of a dozen, but nothing seemed to feel right to Deedee. Jobie marveled at Bachrach's patience. She expected him to be some sort of temperamental genius, but he was charming, engaging Deedee in teasing banter between songs. Jobie thought that he was probably half in love with Deedee, too.

Bachrach turned his empty leather portfolio case upside down and shook it. "That's the lot. We've put these three aside as possibles." He gestured toward a thin stack beside him on the piano bench. "Dionne has shown some interest in this one, but I can safely give you a week or two to think them over."

Jobie smiled at his subtle unspoken challenge that one of Deedee's competitors might scoop her, at the same time implying he favored Deedee for his work.

"He is nice," replied Deedee, bringing Jobie's attention back to present. "There are one or two that might work, especially if he would agree to come over and direct the orchestra and play at the recording session. The problem is that I have to finish this album before my South

Africa trip, and getting him over to London would complicate matters." Deedee sipped her drink. The fan at the jukebox dropped another coin and picked a bossa nova number off Deedee's album, "Quiet Nights of Quiet Stars."

Jobie took Deedee's hand. "Will you dance with me?"

"To this?"

"Especially to this." She took Deedee's hand and pulled her onto the dance floor and into her arms. Jobie closed her eyes and let the music fill her head and her body. The arrangement was simple, an acoustic guitar kept the sensual Latin beat, and a jazz piano played counterpoint to Deedee's amazing voice. Her tones were breathy and intimate, reminding Jobie of a jazz saxophone.

Jobie felt Deedee's breath on her ear. "Are you with me, or did you go away somewhere?"

Jobie pushed back to look into Deedee's eyes. "Your voice is just so amazing. What do you think when you hear yourself like this?"

"I think about the twenty takes we recorded to get the track passable, and I wonder whether we should have done just one more."

Jobie pulled her close again. "You really know how to kill a mood. So, next time I try to seduce you with music, I'll pick someone else's."

"Consider me seduced." Deedee entwined their fingers and wrapped both her arms around Jobie's body, pulling her even closer as they swayed together through the last mellow echoes of the guitar.

Back at their table, Jobie picked up Deedee's empty glass. "Another?"

"Let's go home."

Jobie's stomach tingled. Deedee's unspoken message was clear. She felt as turned on as Jobie, and anxious to be alone together.

Outside L's, at the late hour, MacDougal Street was quiet. Deedee took Jobie's arm. They turned north through Washington Square Park toward Jobie's apartment. Along the brick pathway, streetlights threw down pools of yellow.

"I have to go home tomorrow."

"Already?" Jobie was disappointed but not surprised. She expected that Deedee would be anxious to get back to London to finish her album and get ready for her South Africa tour.

Deedee seemed to read Jobie's thoughts. "Are you sure you won't go with me to Cape Town? Your record company sent you to London. How do you know they won't think your singing in South Africa would be a good idea? You could at least ask."

Jobie wanted to say that she'd try, but she still hesitated, unsure about the politics in South Africa. She'd be labeled as colored by the government's definition, and she suspected there would be restrictions on her traveling there. "I'm not even sure the government would let me in."

"I'll get Kate to work on that side of it, if you're willing to approach Vanguard about going." Deedee stopped them in the dark between two streetlights, took Jobie's face in her hands, and kissed her softly. "Will you?"

Pushing down her hesitation, Jobie nodded.

Chapter Twenty-two

THE BRITISH OVERSEAS AIRWAYS Boeing 707 jet circled over Table Bay on the way to landing at Cape Town airport. The sensation of losing altitude and the change in the sound of the engines woke Jobie. She managed to sleep almost the entire eleven-hour nonstop flight from Heathrow. Jobie opened her eyes and looked directly into Deedee's face, sitting next to her. At some point during the flight, Jobie wasn't sure how she missed it, Deedee had put on her makeup and one of her platinum wigs. She looked ready to greet the press once they landed.

Jobie self-consciously wiped her lips to make sure she hadn't drooled all over herself. "Have you been watching me sleep this whole time? How did you crawl across me to get made-up without waking me?"

Deedee chuckled. "You were sleeping like the dead. I can't ever sleep on a plane. I have the irrational idea that I must stay awake to hold us up by the armrests. Keeps us from falling out of the sky. To tell the truth, I don't fully believe that man can fly."

"You poor thing. I can imagine with your need to control everything, even the physics of flight, your nerves get a workout."

"Yes, and my arms are getting very tired holding up the plane." Deedee looked out the window. "It appears to have worked. We're about to land safely. You're welcome." She squeezed Jobie's hand.

The jet's wheels hit the tarmac, bounced once, and then settled into a straight-ahead taxi down the runway. Kate was with them on the trip acting as a combination manager and show producer. As soon as the seat belt light went out, she jumped up from her seat across the aisle and began getting bags down from the overhead bins.

Jobie barely had time to run a comb through her hair and freshen her lipstick, which wouldn't matter so much. She wouldn't be the focus of the reporters who were sure to be waiting to meet the plane. Jobie's record label had nixed her idea of performing in Cape Town. They felt it was too big a risk for her and not worth the potential of a political incident. Deedee wouldn't settle for no. She listed Jobie as part of her entourage, some kind of unspecified assistant, and paid for Jobie's trip herself.

Kate hustled Deedee and Jobie out of their seats and toward the plane's front door. Marilyn, Peggy, and Betty, Deedee's backup singers, and her five band members followed behind. Jobie paused at the top of the stairs to smell the fresh ocean-scented air that blew across the airfield. In December, the Mediterranean climate of Cape Town was warm, breezy, and dry. To the right she could see Table Mountain, with its distinctive vertical cliffs and flat-topped summit. A thin strip of cloud hung over the top and spilled down the sides, reminding Jobie of the white lace tablecloth that draped her grandmother's dining table in Jasper, Tennessee.

They descended the steps of the plane as flashbulbs popped, and a gaggle of journalists rushed forward and stuck microphones in Deedee's face. Jobie stood at the side with Kate and watched as a poised and pleasant Deedee answered questions about her upcoming shows at the Cape Town Tivoli Theater, her new album, and what brought her to South Africa.

Kate and Jobie watched reporters and photographers jostle each other for access to Deedee. Kate let the interviews go on for a time before stepping behind Deedee and herding her toward the terminal with the reporters trailing. Deedee stopped and looked over her shoulder for Jobie, waited for her to catch up, and took her arm.

"So far, the only thing different is the accents. Have you noticed that all airports in the world look exactly alike?"

Kate rushed them through customs and into a limousine waiting at the curb outside the terminal. "You go on to the hotel, and I'll arrange for the luggage and band's instruments."

Deedee embraced Kate through the open window of the limo and gave her a quick kiss on the mouth just as another flashbulb popped. "What would we do without you?"

The car drove south along the Atlantic, past rows of ice-cream-colored beach huts lined up along the high tide mark, and then turned inland through suburban residential streets. Deedee pointed to the whitewashed houses. "This looks more like Amsterdam than Africa."

The Ritz Plaza Hotel was in the middle of Cape Town's shopping and business sector. Six lanes of traffic bisected the downtown district in front of the hotel. Deedee, Jobie, and the backup singers piled out of the car onto a red carpet leading to massive glass front doors. Jobie caught Marilyn's eye and motioned toward a brass plaque beside the door. It said, "Rights of Admission Reserved." She and Marilyn were the two in the party likely to be restricted and Jobie braced herself for a scene at the front door or at the desk, but the uniformed doorman held the heavy doors open with a perfectly blank face. Once they were in the lobby, the hotel manager rushed over to shake Deedee's hand and to personally escort them to their rooms.

Jobie unpacked and laid out her cosmetics and toiletries in the bathroom. There was a soft knock on her door. When she opened it, Deedee charged her, drove her into the room, and knocked her flat on her back on the bed with Deedee on top.

"Hey!" Jobie said. "I was afraid you might be the Rights of Admission police. Did you see that plaque beside the front door of the hotel?"

"Yes, I saw the sign, but we're not going to stand for any of that nonsense. Don't worry. Kate has put the government on notice."

Jobie wasn't so sure. "I hope you're right."

"You're such a Gloomy Gus. Let's get dressed up and go out on the town."

"Oh, no. You should get a good night's sleep, especially since you didn't sleep at all on the plane. You have rehearsals all day tomorrow, then the show at seven." Jobie didn't say that she was unsure about being out in public with Deedee in Cape Town.

"Aren't you being just the perfect assistant?" She tweaked Jobie's nose. "It does feel wonderful to be prone." Deedee slipped off Jobie, snuggling against her side, and kicked off her shoes. "Especially next to you."

"That's nice. Did you notice a photographer at the airport? Just as we got in the limo. I think he took a photo of you kissing Kate."

"He did?"

"Doesn't that worry you?"

"Not right now."

"Exactly why did you kiss her on the mouth like that?"

There was no response. Deedee was sound asleep and didn't budge even when room service delivered Jobie's dinner.

***

The Cape Town Tivoli Theater was an ornate movie house built in the 1920s to show silent films. The theater was designed to accommodate stage shows, too, with an orchestra pit, and to the right of the stage, a giant pipe organ.

Jobie sat in the empty front row at rehearsal and watched while the band set up their equipment and the backup singers looked over their scores, chatted, and smoked. Deedee and Kate talked with the local light and sound technicians about exactly how Deedee wanted the show produced. Jobie was too far away to hear their words, but from Deedee's gestures she could tell that she wasn't satisfied with the head technician's plan for the lighting. Kate was trying to mediate. She pushed Deedee gently away and stepped between her and the tech. She put her arm around his shoulders and walked him away from Deedee. Marilyn was also watching the exchange. She went over to Deedee and engaged her in a conversation about the score.

Kate and Marilyn were tag-teaming Deedee to keep her calm ahead of the show and help her get the technical arrangements the way she knew she wanted them. Maybe Kate was right; Deedee needed a full-time manager, especially one with production skills like Kate's.

The band finished their setup and started to run through the show's playlist. The first half would be songs from Deedee's successful first album, then an intermission, then the second half, tunes from her new album, slated to be released in the UK in two weeks.

Marilyn and the other backup singers joined the band in their rehearsal, and finally Deedee stepped to the front of the stage and took the microphone. She was halfway through an upbeat number when she suddenly motioned the band to stop. She stared toward the back of the hall. Jobie turned to follow her line of sight. There were two men dressed in grey suits and carrying briefcases coming down the center aisle. They walked to the edge of the stage and pulled identification from their inside coat pockets. Jobie went to stand next to them, close enough to see that they were holding official-looking government IDs.

The taller one spoke. "Miss O'Gwinn?"

"Yes," Deedee answered. She looked over her shoulder to locate Kate, who came rushing from the wing and stood next to Deedee.

"Is there somewhere we can talk?" he asked.

"Talk about what?" asked Kate.

"Take a break, fellows," Deedee said to the band and the singers. She turned back to the two men. "This is my manager, and that's my assistant." She pointed to Jobie. "We can talk right here." She sat down on the edge of the stage.

The man shrugged, as though to say, "Suit yourself." He set his briefcase on the edge of the stage and took out a manila folder. "This is your contract for your performances in Cape Town tonight and tomorrow night. There has been a mistake. We've made the necessary corrections for your signature so that you can get on with your shows without any interruptions." He held out the folder to Deedee.

Kate intercepted it. "What corrections?" She opened the folder and began thumbing through the pages.

"Instead of one show each night, you'll be doing two, separate shows for whites and blacks. Since the tickets have already been sold, that seems the best solution for correcting the mistake."

Jobie held her breath, waiting for the angry explosion she expected from Deedee.

Deedee took the folder from Kate's hand. "We'll need some time to look this over and consult with our attorneys." Her voice was even and unthreatening. Only someone who knew her well would hear the steely note underneath.

"Of course." The man checked his watch. "Shall we say until four o'clock?" He closed his briefcase. "Oh, one more item." He took another manila folder from his briefcase. "I believe this is a picture of your arrival in Cape Town." He handed it to Deedee. "I'm not showing it to you in an official capacity, just out of courtesy, so that, in case there should be questions, you will be prepared." The man offered his hand to Deedee. "Until four o'clock then."

Deedee, Jobie, and Kate wordlessly watched the two men stride up the aisle and out the double doors at the back of the auditorium. "Bloody hell," Kate said.

"I won't do it. I won't play to an all-white crowd." She threw the new contract toward Kate.

Band members and singers began drifting back on stage to their places. Deedee took her position in front of the microphone. "Let's take up where we stopped."

Jobie helped Kate pick up the scattered pages of the contract. "What are you going to do?"

"Right now, I'm going to call the record company in London and get them to speak to the British Consulate here in Cape Town to insist they intervene. You heard Deedee. She's not going to play to an all-white crowd."

Jobie felt a little better, hearing that Kate had a plan. "What's in the second folder?"

Kate opened the folder and held it out to Jobie. It was a grainy photo of Deedee leaning out of the window of a limo, planting a kiss on Kate's lips.

"Oh, no."

Kate shook her head. "Don't worry about the photo yet. If they wanted to put that out, it would be in the newspaper already."

"Thank goodness they didn't photograph her kissing me. It would be on the front page."

Kate headed toward the backstage telephone. "Let's get this contract business settled first, then we can worry about the other if we need to."

By three o'clock, the line in front of the Cape Town Tivoli stretched down the block and around the corner. By four, it had quadrupled in length, wrapping around the theater twice. Jobie put on sunglasses and a wide-brimmed hat to make sure she wouldn't be recognized as she walked down the line to scout out the crowd. She came back into the theater to find Kate. "All white."

Kate kept checking the doors at the back of the auditorium. The government representatives gave four o'clock as the deadline for Deedee to sign the amended contract. "The record label attorneys think the Consulate will be able to work things out." Kate's words were confident, but Jobie noticed that her hand shook as she lit a cigarette.

"What will Deedee do if they insist on segregated audiences?" Jobie asked.

"You know as well as I do, she won't play to an all-white audience. If they come back and try to shut down the show, Deedee will not go quietly."

Rehearsal went on without further interruptions. Deedee, Marilyn, and the other backup singers found their dressing rooms around five o'clock and started the transformation from regular girls to made-up, coiffed, sophisticated-looking stage performers.

At 6:30, the doors opened, and the crowd began to pour in. Ushers rushed to check people's tickets and help them find their seats. At first, everyone was white, but as the auditorium filled, black faces began to show up.

Kate and Jobie let out big sighs and hugged each other. "Crisis averted."

"You deserve so much credit, Kate. I don't know what Deedee would have done without your quick action. She really does need you as a full-time manager."

Kate cocked her head and raised her eyebrows in surprise. "Why, thanks, Jobie. I really appreciate that endorsement from you."

Jobie searched for any hint of irony in Kate's thanks, but it seemed genuine.

Kate shook her head. "Still, I won't relax until we have tomorrow night's show behind us and we're on our way back to London."

The show went well. All the work Deedee and Kate put in with the technicians paid off. The production went on without error, and the audience loved Deedee. Starting off with her better-known songs got the crowd in the mood, and the second half of the program, with her new songs from the new album, had the audience on their feet for a full hour.

After the show, Deedee led the noisy group of Jobie and Kate, the singers and the band, into the lobby of the Ritz Plaza Hotel, headed for the bar to celebrate. They stopped short when six men in suits approached Deedee. "Miss O'Gwinn?"

"Yes." Deedee stood taller, preparing for a fight. Kate stepped to her side and slightly in front of her.

"You and your party will be leaving South Africa tomorrow morning. Your visas have been cancelled. We have to ask you to remain here in the hotel until you leave for the airport."

Kate spoke up. "Our Consulate has been in contact with your government."

"Yes, and they are in agreement that your visit with us has become dangerously political. We can't guarantee your safety."

Deedee pushed Kate to the side. "I'm not political at all. I don't know anything about politics. I just believe that anyone who wants to buy a ticket to hear me sing should be able to."

The man looked past Deedee toward the street. "I'd advise you to remember that you and your show people are guests in our country. Enjoy the rest of your evening here in the hotel. You'll find plane tickets in your rooms for your departure tomorrow morning. Goodbye, Miss O'Gwinn." He led the rest of the men out the door.

Kate and Deedee looked at each other. "I can call the record company again or the Consulate directly," Kate said.

"No. Let's get out of this country. See if we can leave tonight."

Chapter Twenty-three

DEEDEE BEING KICKED OUT of South Africa turned into an international news story. She was lauded in Parliament for standing up against the apartheid government policies of segregation. On the other side, she was accused in the South African press of grandstanding and using the incident to advance her own career in the UK and the US, a way to promote her new album.

Deedee seemed puzzled by the whole uproar. She repeated her message in every press interview. She said she was not political, didn't know anything about the political situation in South Africa, but stood for the idea that anyone who wanted to see her sing should be able to.

Whether the publicity helped her album sales marginally was a moot point. The album was a smash hit. It topped the charts in the UK and Deedee was voted Number One Female Vocalist in the country.

Jobie returned to New York, and she and Deedee fell back into their routine of daily early morning phone calls. On a Monday morning, three weeks after the trip to Cape Town, the jangling of her bedside phone woke Jobie even earlier than usual. She fumbled with the receiver, knocking over the alarm clock. As Jobie righted it, she noticed a scrap of paper with a phone number that she had stuck under the edge of the clock. It was Clair's phone number, the one that the folk singer gave her in Newport. Jobie sat up on the edge of the bed. "Hello," she said when she finally got the phone to her ear.

"Jobie, it's your grandmother."

"Mama, what's wrong?"

"Nothing's wrong. Does something have to be wrong for me to call my granddaughter?"

"No, it's just that it's five o'clock in the morning."

"You haven't written me or called in two months. Every time I try to call you, the line's busy or you just don't answer. I'm calling early to be sure to get you."

Jobie heard her grandfather's voice in the background. "Lily, I'm headed out. Tell Jobie I love her."

"How is Papa?"

"He's fine. He's headed out for the store. He says he can't sleep past four o'clock in the morning anyway, so he gets up and walks to the store and starts the coffee. He's got his regulars that come by every morning."

Jobie pictured her grandfather walking through the pre-dawn, sleepy streets of the small town of Jasper, Tennessee, climbing the weathered steps and crossing the wooden porch of his grocery store on Main Street, across from the county courthouse. She felt a lump rise in her throat. "I miss you and Papa."

"Can't you come home for a visit?"

"I've been taking a lot of time off from my music, and my record company is getting upset. I've been traveling. I've been to London and Cape Town since we talked."

"South Africa? Oh, Jobie, isn't that dangerous for you?"

"It was...exciting, as I look back on it. It was a little scary at the time. We got deported. I went with my new friend, Deedee O'Gwinn. She's a British pop singer. You may have seen the story in the newspaper."

"I don't think I would have paid much attention to a story about Cape Town, South Africa. Tell me about your new friend."

Her grandparents had known Jobie was gay since high school. Growing up, she had both boy and girl friends, but in junior high, puberty struck, and the difference between boys and girls began to assert itself. Her friends paired off in couples, and Jobie became a loner, spending her time in her bedroom reading books, drawing, and teaching herself to play the guitar. She was different. Her parents were really her grandparents. Her crushes were on other girls. She had no interest in being a cheerleader. Jasper, Tennessee was not the place for her. The week after high school graduation, she boarded a bus to New York.

"You say she's a singer too?" Her grandmother rarely brought up the topic of her dating. In the first years of her being in New York, Jobie was too busy getting her singing career off the ground to have more than a few casual relationships. Her grandmother was anxious to know that she wasn't lonely. Jobie didn't want to raise her grandmother's expectations about Deedee. And if she were truthful with herself, she was struggling to manage her own expectations, too.

"Come home for a visit and bring her with you."

Jobie chuckled, picturing Deedee in small town Tennessee. "She lives in London, Mama."

"Even better. I'll bet she could use some good old Southern American cooking."

"We'll see." They chatted a few minutes longer, and Jobie promised to be better about calling. "My international travel is over for a while. I'm playing for a few weeks at Café Wha? here in the Village."

That evening, carrying her guitar case, Jobie walked the five blocks from her apartment to Café Wha?. She strolled south on MacDougal past Washington Square Park on the left and New York University on the right. Jobie always marveled at how different the Village felt from other neighborhoods in New York City. The buildings were low, and she could actually see the sky. The pace of life seemed slower. There were fewer cars and more bicycles on the streets.

The club, on the corner of MacDougal and Minetta, had opened in the late fifties and was one of the original "basket houses" for folk music in the Village, meaning that musicians performed without pay except for what patrons threw in a passed basket after their performance. The practice always reminded Jobie of the passing of the collection plate at the New Zion Baptist Church in Jasper she and her grandparents attended every Sunday morning. Her grandfather always put the money in Jobie's hand so she could be the one to carefully place it in the plate.

Café Wha? was the club Bob Dylan played on his first night in New York. As his reputation grew, his shows in the low-ceilinged, poorly lit subterranean cavern were packed with NYU students, Village residents, and tourists. The buzz among the younger folk singers trying to make their own names was that you never wanted to follow Dylan on the program; when the basket was passed for the young performers that came after, all the patrons were out of money. In recent years, several of the more popular clubs had become successful enough to charge a cover and pay performers. When Jobie rose to becoming a headliner, she was relieved that she wouldn't be passing a basket in Café Wha?, taking money out of younger artists' pockets.

Jobie was surprised to see a block-long line of patrons already waiting in front of the entrance to the club. She stopped to sign a few autographs. Beside the door, a chalkboard notice caught her eye. "Surprise performance, tonight only. The hottest folk group in the country, live on stage. THE TRAVELERS."

Jobie chuckled at the coincidence of finding Clair's phone number that morning and now the prospect of seeing her in the club. Then a saying of her grandmother's jumped into her head. "Coincidences are corrections that God makes to the road you've chosen."

She descended the narrow stairs, steadying herself with her free hand on the brick wall while her eyes adjusted to the dim lighting. Across the large dining-hall-like room filled with chairs and tables, on a small stage at the front sat Clair, Mel, and Don with their heads close together. They were working out the harmonies on a song Jobie hadn't heard before. She took a chair halfway into the room and watched.

Jobie thought back to the evening on the terrace of the Vanderbilt mansion in Newport. Don joked that he was the only one of the three who could sing harmony, and he did appear to be taking the lead in working out the parts for each of them. His voice had the range to sing with Clair's contralto and also with Mel's bass. When they seemed to have the parts worked out, they went through a verse *a cappella*, and Jobie applauded enthusiastically, walking toward the trio on the stage.

Mel and Don greeted Jobie and Clair stepped down from the stage and hugged her. "Did you see the sign out front? We're opening for you tonight."

"I did. I'm honored."

"We're working out some new numbers, as you heard just now, and we wanted a real audience's reaction. Manny is brave enough to let us use his club for that tonight. Okay with you?"

"Of course. My pleasure. Did you see the line out front? The word has gotten out."

Clair and Jobie leaned against the edge of the stage while Mel and Don sat together on a piano bench trying out chords on their guitars. Clair tucked her hair behind an ear. "I hoped I might hear from you after Newport."

"I've kept your number. In fact, I was just looking at it this morning."

"It must be fate that we're seeing each other. So, shall we give ourselves up to the Universe's plan and go to dinner after the show tonight?"

"How can we argue with the Universe?"

"Great. Just great. Have you been to the Coach House?"

"That's right across the street from my apartment."

"I thought so." Clair rushed on to say, "I hope you don't think I've been stalking you, but I did ask around to find out where your apartment is. Is that creepy?"

Jobie laughed. "No, I'm flattered."

"Well." Clair turned to look at her two partners. "I'd better get back to it. See you after your set."

"Yes. Great."

Chapter Twenty-four

THE COACH HOUSE RESTAURANT was just off Washington Square in an authentic nineteenth-century carriage house. The building sat on the corner of a former estate, the land long since chopped up for apartment buildings facing the park. As she and Clair stepped in the front door, Jobie looked around the small dining room. A fireplace of rough-hewn stone covered one wall, and the other three walls were brick and wood-paneling, adorned with handsome oil paintings from the 1800s. There were red leather banquettes and brass chandeliers throwing off gentle light.

The owner met Clair and Jobie at the front door, embraced Clair, and shook Jobie's hand. He led them to a secluded table near the fireplace, pulled out each of their chairs, and motioned for the waiter. Jobie let Clair choose a wine and took her lead ordering the restaurant's signature black bean soup and cornbread sticks.

"I'm impressed," Jobie said.

A small smile played around Clair's mouth. "About?"

"After a show, I'm used to grabbing food standing up at a hole-in-the-wall. This is elegant and it seems to me we're getting the royal treatment. You must come here often."

"When I want to impress someone."

The waiter brought two steaming bowls of soup with aromatic cornbread on the side. "This soup is fantastic, and the cornbread tastes like what my grandmother makes, which is high praise. Most of what I've tasted in the North is Yankee cornbread."

"What's Yankee cornbread?"

"It's sweet. For some reason you Yankees think you're supposed to put sugar in it." Jobie shook her head in disbelief.

"I hear your accent now. I hadn't heard it before you started critiquing our cornbread. Where are you from?"

"Just outside Chattanooga, Tennessee. What about you?"

"Believe it or not, I was born and raised right here in the Village. I went to the Little Red School House, just down the street."

The waiter appeared again and refilled their wine glasses. The wine, the warmth from the fireplace, and a full stomach from the comfort food were working together to lull Jobie into a dreamy, relaxed state. She watched Clair tuck her silky, almost liquid-looking silvery hair behind her ear. Jobie wished she had her sketchbook. She began to mentally draw the outlines of Clair's profile with its distinctive prominent nose.

"Are you staring at me?"

"I'm sorry. I'm being rude. I was mentally sketching you."

"You're an artist as well as a singer?"

"Yes. Maybe you'll sit for me sometime. I've thought about sketching you since we met that night in Newport. You have the most interesting face."

"I would certainly do that if only as an excuse to see more of you. I was so excited when the boys told me we were going to open for you at the Wha? so I'd be sure to see you even though you hadn't called."

"I've been out of town, to South Africa."

"South Africa. That must be quite a story."

"It is. Do you remember I told you about someone I met in London?"

Clair nodded.

"She's Deedee O'Gwinn, the British pop singer. Do you know her?"

"I know of her. Wasn't she in the news recently? Didn't she take a stand against apartheid in Cape Town?"

"I was with her in Cape Town. We got deported."

Clair leaned back in her chair. "Wow. Now I'm the one who's impressed."

Jobie was happy that she had impressed Clair, but felt she needed to set her straight about Deedee's intentions and her own involvement. "I was just along for the ride. I wasn't performing. And Deedee would deny that she was making any kind of political statement. In fact, she has denied it in every interview afterward. She had a contract that said she would not appear in front of segregated audiences, and then when we got there, the police changed the rules. That rubbed her the wrong way."

"Whatever her intentions, she shone a spotlight on conditions that need to change. Other entertainers are going to follow her example, no doubt, refusing to go along with the oppressive regime's rules about segregated audiences. We've certainly never been willing to play there. And you were brave to even go there. You couldn't have known what the government's reception would be of you."

"I didn't. But Deedee was so sure it would all work out. She can be very persuasive."

Jobie traced the edge of a rose embroidered in the white linen tablecloth. "I'm not very passionate about political causes, either." She looked up at Clair. "Does that make you think less of me?"

Clair shook her head. "No, you're young yet. That may change." She paused as the waiter refilled both their wineglasses. "So, I guess things have moved along between you and Deedee, romantically I mean." She looked into Jobie's eyes. The flickering fire reflected in her gaze.

Jobie hesitated. "Yes, I think so. Living so far apart complicates matters. We're separated by thirty-five hundred miles, and we're both so busy. I've never been in a serious relationship, so I don't have any way to know for sure how it's supposed to go."

"I'd hate to have to generalize about how relationships are supposed to go, but I've had some personal not-so-good experience with a long-distance affair."

"It didn't work out?"

"No." Clair stared into the fire. Jobie waited for her to go on. "The distance between us was a problem. She was in Los Angeles, but more important was that we had different expectations about where we were going with the relationship. At a certain point, I was ready to be exclusive, and she wasn't, so we called it off. It was amicable."

Jobie pictured Deedee on the sofa in her apartment telling her that Kate wanted a commitment that she wasn't willing to give. Jobie leaned toward Clair. "Doesn't everyone want that kind of promise from someone they care about?"

"Everyone? Maybe not. I think it often depends on timing and circumstances and your shared values. The worst thing is to have unspoken expectations."

"How did you get so smart about this?"

"Bitter experience and self-preservation, my dear. 'Those who don't learn from history are doomed to repeat it.'"

"Ugh. It sounds like so much work. What about romance and spontaneity and being swept away with the emotions of love?"

"All wonderful." Clair raised her glass. "Somehow I've gotten on the wrong side of this conversation. I'm really a hopeless romantic, or maybe more accurately, a hopeful romantic. Here's to romance, and let's change the subject. How's your music going?"

"My record label is after me right now to do a college tour. They say they can line up a dozen dates and that the exposure would sell lots of albums."

"They're right about that, but you sound reluctant."

Jobie squirmed in her chair. "It's just not my thing. I've seen you, Mel, and Don in front of big audiences. You relate so well to them."

Clair nodded. "We do. I think it's easier with three of us. Mel keeps track of the playlist. He has it taped to his guitar. Don tells the jokes. All I have to worry about is staying on key and remembering the lyrics."

"So, do you think I should do the tour?"

"I just know that the college audiences are important for us, with popular music the way it is today." Clair sipped her wine and glanced at Jobie. "I'll admit, I had hoped to see more of you, and I'd feel conflicted about your being gone on tour for several weeks, now that we're becoming acquainted. But it sounds like I'm losing out to Deedee anyway, before I even get started."

I guess it does sound that way to her, though Deedee and I certainly haven't had much time to talk about the future.

Clair put her hand on Jobie's. "I'm sorry. The look on your face tells me that comment sounded out of left field."

"No. I'm thinking about what you said about having unspoken expectations. Deedee and I have never had much time to talk about where we're going."

"Timing is everything. Trust yourself to know when. Anyway, about the college tour, which is where this conversation started, if I'm being objective, it sounds like a good idea."

After dinner, Clair walked with Jobie the two short blocks to her apartment through the quiet late-night streets of Greenwich Village. They stopped in front of the steps. "Here we are. Will you come in?"

"Better not, I guess."

Jobie sat on the bottom step, hoping to prolong the time with Clair. "Because of Deedee?"

Clair sat beside her. "I don't feel that complicating things for you would be a good idea. Besides, I've sworn off drama as a way of life. Too exhausting. I do hope we can see each other again."

"Of course. I promise not to spend the whole evening talking about another woman next time."

Clair pulled Jobie to her feet, held her shoulders, and leaned in and kissed her chastely, as she had the first time on the terrace in Newport.

Jobie was disappointed that she wouldn't get the opportunity to heat up Clair's cool kiss. It felt like a challenge.

Clair chuckled, and Jobie wondered if her thoughts showed on her face. "Goodnight, Jobie."

Jobie climbed the steps to her apartment and passed up turning on the light in the living room. She stood at the window in the dark watching Clair cross the street into the park. In the glow reflected from a streetlight, Clair turned and waved. She appeared confident Jobie would be watching from the window.

She went through her bedtime routine on autopilot. She shrugged into one of the ancient oversized tee shirts that she slept in and crawled between the covers with a book. She read the same paragraph three times before she gave up on being able to concentrate. She was running over in her head what Clair said about long-distance relationships and unspoken expectations.

If she and Deedee were to be together, would Jobie have to make the move to London? Would Deedee consider moving to New York? Did Deedee even feel the need to be closer together, or was she still satisfied with the early morning phone calls and infrequent meetings in person? And would she ever be willing to make a commitment to being exclusive? Jobie imagined the scores of women throwing themselves at Deedee. She remembered the woman in L's flirting with Deedee, and Deedee's response even though Jobie was right there. Then there was always Kate. She was as close to Deedee as anyone could be, and Deedee admitted she had a history with Kate. Jobie remembered the kiss that Deedee gave Kate from the limo.

She resolved to bring up the discussion about finding a way of being together with Deedee during their next early morning call and turned off the bedside lamp.

***

Deedee called earlier than usual the next morning. She sounded breathless with excitement. "I'm sorry for calling you so early. I've been sitting here tapping my foot and drumming my fingers, but I couldn't wait any longer. Guess what."

"I don't have a clue." Jobie fluffed up her pillow and leaned against the headboard.

"The BBC has offered me my own TV show. It will be on every week for an hour, and I get to choose my own music and guests, and they'll hire Kate as the producer. They said I can do anything, the more eclectic the better. We'll have a generous budget for costumes and sets and backup musicians and singers."

Jobie couldn't help feeling ambivalent. Of course, this was wonderful news for Deedee. It sounded as though the network was willing to give her a high level of artistic control, which was so important to Deedee. Having Kate with her made it even better. With one show, Deedee could reach a bigger audience than with a hundred concerts. It would be a built-in way to promote her records. But with a weekly TV show in London, there was no way Deedee could consider being with Jobie in New York. If the show was a hit, it might run for years.

"Jobie. Are you there?"

"Yes, I'm here. That's wonderful news. You're going to be a huge hit."

"I'll be hugely busy, that's for sure. If we get the deal signed next week, we'll start pre-production the week after."

Deedee chattered on, talking about who she was thinking of for guests. She ticked off a wide-ranging list from Woody Allen to The Beatles to Cilla Black. "And of course, Martha and the Vandellas and Marvin Gaye and The Supremes. I could do a whole show on the Motown sound. I should be writing all this down so I can talk to Kate about it." She stopped. "What am I thinking? I called and woke you before dawn, and I'm rattling on. I'm sorry. I miss you so much. Tell me what's going on with you."

"I had dinner last night at a wonderful restaurant. I wish you could have been with me."

"Who was with you?"

"Clair Ruffin. She's the girl singer with the Travelers."

"Oh, I know who she is. She's a knockout. Should I be jealous? Who invited who?"

"We sort of invited each other. I think. I met her at the Newport Folk Festival. We were both at the Café Wha? last night."

"Did she make a pass at you?"

"No." Jobie drew out the word. "In fact, we spent most of the time talking about you. She was impressed by your stand against apartheid in Cape Town." Jobie tucked the phone between her ear and shoulder and began to get dressed. "I have news, too. The label wants me to do a college tour, and I think I'll do it." As she spoke the words, she made up her mind to agree to the tour. "They're thinking about a dozen schools, two shows a week."

"You don't sound that excited."

Jobie sat on the edge of the bed to pull on her jeans. "I'm not. You know me. I'm happiest in coffee houses right here in the Village, but they expect the exposure to boost my album sales."

Deedee was quiet on the other end of the line.

"Are you there?" said Jobie.

"Yes." Deedee laughed. "Do you notice we keep having to ask each other that?"

"It's hard. Just being on the phone. And I'm acutely aware that these international calls cost you a fortune."

"Hearing your voice is worth every quid. If you're on tour and I'm busy as hell with a TV show, we're going to have an even harder time connecting. I don't like the prospect of that. As I was dialing this morning, I imagined how great it would be if you came over to London. We had fun in Cape Town, even with the problems. I loved having you with me. You would be a big help now, with the TV show and all."

Jobie was encouraged that Deedee was feeling a desire to be together, but did she really believe—as she sounded—that her career was more important than Jobie's? This was another example of how being so far apart was frustrating. Jobie wished she were able to see Deedee's body language. She wanted to hang up before she became angry. "I have to go."

They chatted a bit longer. Jobie promised to write from the road as often as possible, since they both would likely be too busy for daily calls.

Jobie hung up the phone and sat on the edge of the bed, searching her mind to find reasons to be excited about a college tour. She might have a chance to do some sketching, during down times, of the new places she'd be seeing. She would insist on one of the stops being close to Jasper so she could visit her grandparents. But a thought intruded and darkened her mood. She couldn't see any time in the future when she and Deedee would be able to spend more time together.

Chapter Twenty-five

JOBIE FOLLOWED THE SIDEWALK that edged the quad area, past the chapel where she had played a concert the night before. She felt conspicuous, but not because she was older than the students who passed her on their way to classes or lounged on the grass under oak trees. She was only twenty-two, not much of an age difference. It was her clothes and looks that made her feel different. She wore her usual jeans, sandals, and peasant blouse. All the male students wore long-sleeved white dress shirts and ties, and the girls wore skirts.

Jobie had insisted that Sewanee, the name of the small Tennessee town where University of the South was located and the nickname of the school itself, would be the last stop on the tour her record company put together. It was only fifty miles from Jasper. She was looking forward to visiting her grandmother and grandfather after the two shows she was scheduled to play.

She spent the night in a charming cottage on campus. The school sat in the middle of nowhere, surrounded by 13,000 acres of woods, streams, and outcroppings of limestone boulders. The four-color glossy brochure beside her bed told the history of the school. It was a private liberal arts school, founded by conservative Episcopalians in 1858 just before the Civil War on the principle that they wanted a place of higher learning that was "free of Northern influences." In other words, Jobie thought, they wanted to turn out graduates who believed in the rights of white citizens in the Southern states to own slaves.

She hadn't been sure the students of this conservative school would accept her music. Many of her songs were freedom anthems and decidedly anti-war. She was pleasantly surprised. The record label and the promoters purposefully sited the concert in the chapel rather than the school's field house. It was a smaller and more intimate venue. They felt certain that she could fill it. They were right. Last night's show, the first one, was sold out and standing room only, and the crowd's reception was enthusiastic. Maybe things were really changing, even in the traditional old South.

The morning after the show, she had breakfast in the communal dining room with the students and set out with her sketch pad under her arm. She was looking forward to trying to get the beauty of the wild surroundings down on paper. Off the sidewalk, she took a gravel path that led across a stream and into the woods. She wandered along the path for twenty minutes until she came to an area where the trees parted on her right to reveal a huge boulder that formed a perfect perch for looking out over the valley below. She carefully climbed up on the rock on all fours and settled down to draw.

As she sketched, the sun rose high across the clear blue sky until noon, then began to move toward the horizon on her left. Jobie was lost in her work, carried away by the breathtaking vista that unfolded below her.

"Wow. That's beautiful," a voice behind her said.

Jobie started with surprise, almost losing her balance on top of the rock. A steadying hand held her while the other hand reached out and caught the sketch pad as it slid off the rock.

"Sorry. I wasn't sneaking up on you. I thought you must have heard me." The girl stepped around into Jobie's field of vision. She wore jeans with the cuffs rolled up over boots and a short-sleeved green shirt with the Sewanee logo appliquéd over the left breast pocket. Her curly dark brown hair was cut short, and her dark eyes matched its color.

She held the sketch pad at arm's length and studied Jobie's work. "I've seen a lot of people climb up here and try to capture the beauty of these woods with paint or cameras. You're the best so far."

"Thank you."

The young woman handed the sketch pad back to Jobie. "Aren't you the folk singer?"

"Yes. Who are you?"

"Oh, I'm the Domain Manager." She stuck her hand out. "Cindy."

"Jobie." Jobie crawled down from the boulder and shook Cindy's hand. "What's a Domain Manager?"

Cindy laughed and nodded. "We call these thirteen thousand acres the Domain." She made a sweeping gesture that took in the woods and valley. "I'm responsible for land management decisions across the Domain."

"How do you become the Domain Manager?"

Cindy shrugged. "I have an MS in wildlife biology and forestry, and I was in the right place at the right time. You're thinking I'm too young, right? I get that a lot. Don't people say that about you, too?"

"Yes, but I'm just responsible for myself, not for decisions about thirteen thousand acres."

Cindy leaned against the boulder. "I guess. Anyway, I saw your show last night, and I love your music. My grandpa used to tease me by saying I couldn't carry a tune in a bucket. He played the fiddle when he was young, but he was too busy trying to support his family to do much with it. We found his fiddle in the attic when he died, and I have it. But I could never play it. So, which is your true passion, folk singing or painting?"

"I'd love to spend more time on my painting but singing pays the bills. With the singing, I was in the right place at the right time, like you with your domain management."

"Don't some people, if they're good, pay the bills with their art?"

"Some people do make a living with their art, of course. I've just never been confident enough in my talent to take the chance. And singing has come so easily. I went to New York after high school, and my music caught on faster than my art. That's my home now."

"Where were you raised? You sound like you're from around here."

"I was raised in Jasper."

"Oh, close to here."

"Yes. I'm going there tomorrow to visit my grandparents."

"Do you ever miss Tennessee? Living in New York?"

"I didn't fit in very well in Jasper."

"I feel that way sometimes, but I have only one passion, and there aren't very many domains to manage in New York. Not much wildlife, I'd guess."

"Pigeons and squirrels."

"Right. Well, I'd better get going. A student reported there's a rockslide blocking the trail a little farther along. I'm on my way to check it out. Good to meet you, Jobie."

"Yes, I have to get back soon. I have the show tonight."

"I know, I'm planning to see you again." Cindy started off at a trot down the trail. She stopped and turned back toward Jobie. "Sing good." She pantomimed playing the fiddle and waved goodbye.

Jobie climbed up on the rock again. She wanted to take as much advantage of the light as possible before she started back to the main campus to prepare for her second show. As she worked over her drawing, she thought about the question Cindy asked, whether art or music was her true passion. If she focused on her art, she would have to spend her full time building up an inventory of works that she might, just might, be able to get placed in a gallery. How would she live in New York in the meantime? She could move back home to Jasper,

Tennessee, but what about Deedee? And where did things really stand with Deedee? There didn't seem to be easy answers to any of these questions. She looked out over the Domain, as Cindy called it. The hills and valleys, with their solid deep green canopy of trees, were as still and silent as the drawing she was working over. Better to just take things one at a time, and the next priority was her show tonight. She climbed down and headed back to the campus.

Chapter Twenty-six

JOBIE SAT AT THE white enameled metal kitchen table, struggling to peel apples while her grandmother made pie dough. "Clearly skill at peeling apples isn't genetic. You're so good at it, and I'm so bad." The knife slipped from Jobie's hand and bounced off the linoleum floor. "I used to watch fascinated while you peeled a whole apple in seconds with one long unbroken string."

Lily looked over her shoulder and smiled. "Practice."

Jobie leaned to retrieve the knife and held up a section of apple skin. "Look at this, I'm leaving more apple on the peel than on the apple."

"Don't throw those peelings away. I'll make applesauce with them."

Jobie blew a stray lock of hair out of her eye. "I was so excited to see you and Papa waiting for me at the bus. Do you remember that you stood on the same spot to see me off for New York four years ago?"

"Of course, I remember."

Jobie laid the knife on the table and flexed her fingers. "It was raining. You chased after the bus as long as you could keep up with it, crying the whole time. I was so excited about starting a new life that I didn't realize how traumatic that was for you. Do you forgive me?"

"Yes. I knew you had to get out into the world, even if it was hard on us."

Jobie gazed around the kitchen, so familiar to her after living there her first eighteen years. "You haven't asked me yet how long I can stay. That's always the first thing you ask when I come home."

"I've been dying to, but you and Papa always tease me when I do. I'm trying not to appear so needy. But how long can you stay?"

Jobie laughed. "I'm planning to stay a week."

"Only a week?"

Jobie nodded. "I've been gone on this tour for a long time. I have to get back."

Lily stepped to the refrigerator and returned to the mixing bowl with a light-yellow brick of butter. The stoneware bowl that she was working over was a relic from the eighteenth century, passed down through generations of women in her family. Jobie watched her grandmother cut the cold butter into the flour with a fork, leaving tiny pearls of fat that would melt in the oven to make the flaky crust her grandmother was so proud of.

"Will Papa come home from the store for lunch?"

"Since you're here, probably. He usually keeps the store open all day right through lunchtime. He's concerned someone may need something and not be able to get it." Lily glanced out the screen door. "Even if he has to step away for a minute, he leaves the door open and puts a sign and a coffee can by the cash register, telling people to take what they need and put their money in the can."

"And he trusts people to do that?"

Lily nodded. She dusted her rolling pin with flour and began shaping the dough into a pie crust. "When she was a little girl, your mother loved watching me work with the dough. She would stand on her knees in the chair where you're sitting right now. I'd give her a pinch of the dough to roll out with a piece of wood dowel that Papa cut for her. She fashioned little cookies in the shapes of animals and sprinkled them with sugar and cinnamon, and I'd bake them for her, along with the pie." Lily stopped her work and stared into space. "She was so good at making those little animals. I always thought she would turn out to be an artist, like you have." She wiped her eyes with the back of her wrist.

"I miss her too, Mama, even though I never knew her."

"I know you do, honey." Lily sat down, took the knife from Jobie, and began to quickly and efficiently peel the apples.

"Tell me about her again."

Lily's knife paused over her work. "Your mother was the image of Papa, in looks and in personality. Sometimes it seemed like she just dropped into my lap from nowhere. I never saw any of my faults reflected in her. She got up happy every morning of her seventeen years. Never had a bad word to say about anyone and never held a grudge. When we found out that you were coming, I was after Papa to call the boy and his parents out. I think I wanted to kill them all, but she wouldn't tell us for sure who the father was. She'd just say it was a white boy she met in town."

"You've always told me you don't know who he was, my father, and I've always believed you'd tell me if you did. You would, wouldn't you?"

Lily put down the apple she was peeling and embraced Jobie. "Of course, we would. She never brought anybody around. For years after you were born, I stared at young white men on the street and in stores, thinking I could recognize one of them in you, but that was silly." She smoothed Jobie's hairline. "After she told us you were coming, she went to stay in Chattanooga with my sister, your great-aunt Martha, until you were born, and we never spoke of the father again. She just started looking forward to you coming. She never complained about the headaches until she was about seven months along, and by the time we got to the hospital the day you were born, the doctors had to bring you into the world early to try and save her life and yours."

Lily wiped her eyes with the bottom of her apron. "My sweet daughter didn't make it. You were tiny, only three and a half pounds, but thank goodness you had a strong set of lungs. Martha and I heard your first cry all the way out in the waiting room. It was more a yell than a cry. I remember we just had to laugh. You sounded surprised to be out in the world so early. Right then I suspected you'd be a singer."

"And you named me after Jobyna Jones. I know you traveled with her show, but you never talk much about that time."

"Oh, honey, that was so long ago. I've crossed many rivers since then, as our old folks used to say."

"I know, but you must have amazing stories to tell, and you must have had a special connection with Jobyna, to name me after her, I mean."

Lily looked up from the apple she was peeling. Her eyes took on a faraway look. Jobie thought she was about to go on and talk about Jobyna. Lily glanced at the clock on the stove. "Oh, goodness, look at the time. Papa will be home any minute, and I've got to get this pie in the oven, and I know y'all will want cornbread."

Lily mixed the cornbread batter and poured it in a black cast-iron skillet she had been heating in the oven. The skillet had been passed down through the family along with the old mixing bowl. She put it in the oven with the apple pie and sat next to Jobie at the table.

Jobie began to collect the apple peelings in a bowl. "Will you teach me to make cornbread? I was explaining to a friend in New York the difference between good cornbread and Yankee cornbread." Jobie got a picture of Clair's profile against the firelight at the Coach House. Could she do a drawing from memory?

"I'll gladly teach you. You never wanted to spend time in the kitchen when you were growing up. You were too busy with your music and your art. Cornbread is easy. The secret is cooking it in a cast-iron skillet, the more seasoned the better. I inherited mine from your great-aunt Martha, God rest her soul, and she inherited it from our mother. No telling where Mother got it."

The two women heard off-key whistling outside followed by footsteps on the back porch. Arthur Greene pulled the screen door open, and Jobie heard the familiar screech of the hinges. "I need to put some oil on that," Arthur mumbled to himself. He was tall and thin, and moved with the grace of a young man even though he was in his sixties. His hair and mustache were grey, but his face was wrinkle-free, except for smile lines at the corners of his sparkling eyes.

Jobie jumped up from the table and threw her arms around his neck. "Please don't put oil on it, Papa. I love that sound. It reminds me of you and Mama and all our mornings in this kitchen."

Arthur chuckled. "Most of the time I don't even hear it. You being home brings it to mind." Arthur joined Jobie at the table. The kitchen began to fill with the mouthwatering smells of baking apples and cinnamon.

"Your Mama and I sometimes sit at this table and wonder if you might ever come back to Jasper, or Chattanooga, to live close to us."

Lily said, "Arthur, don't hector her."

Jobie hugged Arthur again and kissed him on the cheek, feeling the familiar tickle of his mustache on her face. "I don't feel hectored. In fact, I was daydreaming the other afternoon about concentrating full time on my art, living here until I can build up enough works for a show in New York. My recording contract is up in a few weeks."

"Oh, Jobie, if you would do that we'd be overjoyed."

"Even if it meant giving up my singing?"

"You wouldn't have to give it up forever, would you? Papa could make you a studio in the old smokehouse out back. We never use it anymore except for storage. He could put in lots of windows for ventilation and light, and maybe even a skylight. Couldn't you, Papa?"

"I sure could, but won't your record company be after you to sign another contract?"

"They're going to put out a live album from this tour I just finished. I suspect that may be my last one with Vanguard. Folk music isn't as popular as it used to be, at least my folk music. I've got to decide whether to find another label or take a little time off, maybe six months, to build up enough material for a show...I don't know."

Lily took Jobie's hand. "Come home, honey."

"Who's hectoring now?" Arthur touched Lily's cheek.

"I know. You're right. I'm just saying that she's welcome. Whatever you decide, Jobie. Help me get this dinner on the table, you two."

After the meal, Arthur pushed his chair away from the table and patted his belly. "Lily, that was the best meal you've ever cooked."

Lily laughed. "You say that every day, Arthur."

"I know. It's true. Don't know how you do it time after time."

Jobie stood up and began clearing the dishes off the table.

"Honey, why don't you let me take care of those," Lily said. "Go back to the store this afternoon with Papa so the two of you can spend some time together. I hate to think about it, but you'll be saying you have to go back to New York before we know it." Lily turned away quickly and started running water in the sink.

Arthur looked at Lily's back and winked at Jobie. "Yes, that would be nice, Jobie. People in Jasper haven't seen you in a while. I brag about you so often that some of my newer customers may think I've made you up."

Jobie and Arthur went out the back door, crossed the backyard, and turned toward downtown on a well-worn path that ran next to rusty railroad tracks. "I've never known what these tracks were for," Jobie said. "They've never had a train on them during my lifetime. Us kids used to balance on the rails, pretending they were tightropes and we were in the circus. We never worried about a train coming along."

"There used to be a train that ran between Jasper and Chattanooga, but that was way before you were born. There were sawmills around these parts and the big landowners built it to haul logs and milled lumber back and forth. They closed it down once the lumber played out, but they never took up the tracks. Just left them here to rust. I've told you how I rode the train to Chattanooga when I courted your grandmother forty years ago."

"Tell me again, Papa."

Arthur patted her hand, resting in the crook of his arm. "Your grandmother was the prettiest thing I ever saw. She was staying with her sister, your great-aunt Martha, and Carl. I went to school with Martha and Carl, he's my cousin, you know, but Lily was younger. She had come back from being a dancer with a traveling show company. You've seen that picture she has of her in the chorus line?"

Jobie nodded.

"Martha and Carl invited me to Sunday dinner. As I look back, her sister had in mind to put Lily and me together, hoping we'd hit it off."

"And you did."

"Not right away, we didn't. I was very full of myself back then.

Considered myself a catch. I had made a deal with old Mr. Gable to sell me the store where I'd worked since high school. He wanted to move to Knoxville, closer to his daughter. But Lily paid no attention to me the whole time. Put me in my place, and, of course, that made me even more interested in her."

"So how did you win her over?"

"I'm not sure. I just kept after her, riding the train to Chattanooga every Sunday morning, walking a mile and a half out to their place for dinner, then walking back to the train and coming home. Some Sundays she wouldn't even come out of the kitchen. Carl and I sat around on the porch while Lily and Martha made the meal and cleaned up afterward. I just kept coming every week. I think I wore her down."

The path veered away from the railroad tracks and joined up with a sidewalk running along Jasper's Main Street. They walked past the storefronts of Clayton's 5 and 10, Young's Dry Goods, and The Smart Ladies' Apparel Shoppe till they came her grandfather's grocery store. Jobie paused in front and looked up at the porcelain RC Cola sign that hung over the porch with red lettering spelling out Gable's Grocery.

"Why didn't you ever change the name, Papa?"

"Oh, I don't know. Folks were used to Gable's, and we would have had to make a new sign."

On the counter by the cash register was the coffee can and a carefully handprinted sign that declared, BACK SOON. TAKE WHAT YOU NEED. ARTHUR. Arthur picked up the coffee can and sorted the money into the cash drawer.

Jobie shook her head. "I forget how different things are in Jasper than in New York City."

"I suspect Mama sent us off together this afternoon so I could talk you into leaving New York and coming back to Jasper to do your art. You know how she is when her mind gets set on something."

"Do you think I should come back?"

Arthur reached under the counter, pulled out a green apron, and put it on. "You asked me whether you should be in New York four years ago, before you got on the bus to go."

Jobie nodded. "You told me that when you come to a crossroad and you have a choice of two different directions, don't think that one is wrong and the other is right. They're just different. I've thought about that advice often."

Arthur chuckled. "Sounds like I was trying hard not to give you advice."

"I feel guilty sometimes that I don't have enough passion for my music. I don't feel real as a protest singer. There are certainly real things to protest, but other people seem to do it much better than me. But it would be making a big change, dropping my music and taking the time off. I've got something else to consider, too. There's someone I want to spend more time with and she's in London."

The small brass bell over the front door tinkled as a woman came in. She dug in her handbag with one hand for a grocery list while she held on to a toddler with the other. Arthur turned to wait on the woman, and Jobie went to the front window and looked across Main Street toward the courthouse and a pay phone that stood on the corner. She checked her watch and calculated the time difference; 2:30 pm in Jasper meant 7:30 pm in London. Her communication with Deedee had been spotty while she was on tour. Since being in Jasper, she hadn't found time or opportunity to make an international long-distance call. The customer wandered over to the produce bins to inspect the tomatoes while her little girl stared big-eyed at the stick candy in glass jars on the counter.

"Papa, I'm going to run across the square and use the pay phone."

Arthur nodded.

After a long series of clicks and ten rings, Jobie hung up. Finding Deedee at home was a long shot. No need to feel disappointed. She crossed the courthouse lawn to a rack of postcards on the sidewalk outside the drug store and picked one with a picture of Lookout Mountain on the front, then went into the post office two doors down. She bought a stamp and used the pen chained to the counter to write Deedee a message.

Just tried to call you. Finished the tour and am visiting Mama and Papa in Jasper. Call me when you can find time in your busy schedule. I have something important to talk over with you. Remember we're 5 hours earlier. I miss you. Jobie.

She wrote her grandparents' phone number underneath and dropped the card in the outgoing mail slot.

Jobie walked back across the square toward her grandfather's store. She paused to let a mud-spattered pickup truck pass. The farmer at the wheel waved and Jobie stared after him, wondering if he thought he knew her or if he was just being neighborly. Another way the small Tennessee town was different from the big city. She heard a woman's voice behind her. "Jobie? Is it Jobie Greene?" She turned toward the voice and saw a tall, thin woman coming toward her, smiling.

"Mrs. Root." Jobie returned the tight hug the woman gave her. The embrace took Jobie back to tenth grade when Mrs. Root, her high school art teacher, had been her first crush.

Mrs. Root's long, bright fuscia scarf came unwound from her neck with the hugging, and she tossed one end of it back over her shoulder. "My most talented art student ever. Right here in little Jasper again. How are you, Jobie? From the news, you're doing well with your music. I subscribe to the Sunday *New York Times* just so I can keep up with you."

"That means a lot to me. You were a great inspiration to me."

Mrs. Root smiled and took Jobie's hands. "I just remember telling you that it was all right to be different. You were very special. Are very special." She looked across the square to Priestly's Drug Store. "Are you headed somewhere, or do you have time for a Coke? If I remember right, you used to love cherry Cokes at Priestly's."

"Yes. I'd like that."

Mrs. Root took Jobie's arm as they crossed the square in front of the courthouse. On the front door of the drug store in fancy gold script were the words, "Priestley's Drug Store, Est. 1899." Inside on the left was a long marble counter with red-upholstered stools bolted to the black-and-white checkerboard tile floor. Behind the counter, a teenaged soda jerk in a long white apron and starched cap was keeping busy between customers by wiping fingerprints off the chrome sundae-toppings pumps.

Mrs. Root said, "Let's sit in a booth. More private."

She steered Jobie past the counter and a Wurlitzer jukebox that Jobie remembered seeing in the same corner from grade school through junior high and high school. As a child, she was fascinated by the bubbling lights that chased each other up and down the front.

They ordered their drinks and Mrs. Root said, "How long are you here for?"

"I'm just here for a visit at the end of a tour."

"I know. A college tour. As I said, I keep up with your career."

"Actually, Mrs. Root, it's funny I've run into you. I'm thinking of coming home for a few months to focus on my art for a while."

"Can you do that? And do you think you could call me Jean? We're not student and teacher anymore."

Jobie nodded. It would feel awkward addressing her former teacher by her first name, but she determined to try. "Well...Jean...if I'm ever going to make the change, now's the time. All the signs from the Universe are pointing me toward doing it, running into you being one of them. What do you think?"

"I'll admit I'm not entirely objective. I'd love to see you back doing your painting, and maybe see more of you, but I certainly don't know the music business. I'll ask you this question...if you could look into the future and see that interrupting your music career would mean you couldn't go back to it, would you be regretful?"

The jukebox jumped into life with one of Jobie's songs. She turned to see the soda jerk grin and salute her. He came over to their table with a pencil and slip of paper. "An autograph? Do you mind? Make it to James. I'm a big fan. I play the guitar and write music, too." He stuck the paper forward, Jobie took it and signed, and James went away smiling.

"And that part, too. Would you be regretful losing out on the fan recognition?"

"Hmmm." Jobie stirred her cherry Coke with the straw. She looked up. "I don't think I would. I would be more regretful not having tried."

"There's your answer."

Chapter Twenty-seven

THE TELEPHONE HUNG ON the wall in her grandmother's kitchen, where it had always been. When it rang at three o'clock in the morning, the jangling shook Jobie out of a sound sleep. She sat up in bed, disoriented. She fumbled at the foot of the bed for her robe. Before she could find it, her grandfather knocked softly on her bedroom door.

"Jobie, it's for you. She says it's Deedee. From the accent, I'd guess your friend from London."

Jobie padded to the phone barefooted. "Hello, Deedee? What's wrong?"

"Nothing's wrong. Am I calling too early? I just got your card and couldn't wait to hear your voice. Oh, my, it's only three o'clock there. Was that your grandfather who answered? Sorry."

"Give me a second." Jobie rubbed her eyes and pulled a chair over from the kitchen table. "I'm here."

"Kate and I have been crazy busy, working practically twenty-four hours a day. I hardly know what time it is in this time zone, let alone in Tennessee. The show premiers in two weeks, and everything's new from the ground up: the crew, the sets, costumes, cast, the orchestra. Jobie, there's an orchestra and the greenest of all is me. Kate's the only one who knows what she's doing. Thank heaven for her, and Marilyn. There's even a choreographer. Can you believe I have to dance? And there are writers. I have lines to learn every week. I'm too nearsighted to read cue cards, so I have to memorize everything. It's not as though I can hide. The show's called, *DEEDEE!* It's all on me."

Jobie looked across the kitchen, wishing there was a way to start a pot of coffee. She could hang up and call back if it weren't for the international phone charges that would show up on her grandmother's phone bill. "You sound more excited than anxious. You must feel confident that you and Kate are up to the challenges." Jobie felt a prick of jealousy with the lingering concern about Kate's romantic feelings for Deedee and how important she seemed to Deedee's success.

"We don't have any choice. We've negotiated a deal that gives me lots of control, something I've dreamed of with my albums and appearances. So, the pressure comes with the territory."

Jobie wanted to shift the conversation to her possible decision to drop her singing and move back to Jasper for a while. "Can we talk a minute about something I'm struggling with?"

"Of course. I'm sorry I'm running on. It's so good to talk to you, and I've called you without planning enough time. I'm late leaving for the studio already. Kate's pacing like a caged animal."

"Kate's there in your apartment?"

"Yes." Deedee put her hand over the receiver and spoke to Kate. "Sit down for a minute. Or get another cup of tea. You're making me nervous. My notes from last night are on the table there. Look them over for a minute."

"Deedee," said Jobie.

"Sorry. I'm here. I'm here."

Jobie drew a breath and released it before speaking. She needed to talk about the future of their relationship and how it might bear on her possible decision to move back to Jasper, but she wanted to talk when they had more time and she could have Deedee's full attention, without Kate circling around. "Can you call me back when you have more time?"

"Of course. Let's see. One in the morning here will be—"

"Eight o'clock at night here."

"Perfect. I'll call you. I'm sending you a kiss. I have a surprise for you."

Jobie hung up the phone and considered crawling back in bed, but she was sure she wouldn't be able to sleep. A surprise? Could Deedee be planning another spur-of-the-moment visit to the US? Unlikely, since she and Kate were so consumed with the TV show.

She started a pot of coffee, opening and closing cabinets as quietly as possible to avoid disturbing her grandparents again. She looked up to see her grandfather standing in the doorway, dressed and ready to go off to the store.

He walked over to Jobie and hugged her. "Is everything okay, honey?"

"Yes, Papa, just a time zone challenge. I'm sorry we woke you."

"I get up about this time to go to the store anyway. Let's sit here and drink our coffee. Tell me about your new friend in London."

Jobie poured two cups and took them to the table. She told her grandfather about meeting Deedee in the TV studio in London, about her amazing voice, about her career success, and about her new TV show on BBC. "Her talent is huge, but the thing I admire most about her is that she's sure about what she wants and how to get it."

Arthur smoothed the hair away from her face. "Where does she see you fitting in?"

"I don't know yet." She took her grandfather's hand. "How did you know that Mama was the one for you? How have you stayed so happy together for so long?"

"That's easy. I've always wanted her to have the biggest strawberry."

"What do you mean?"

"What makes Lily happy makes me happy. All I have to do is pay attention and listen. I can't keep everything bad away from our lives, but whatever I have control of I'm going to do my best to make her happy."

The swish of Lily's slippers signaled her coming through the hallway to the kitchen. "Good morning, you two." She beamed at her husband and granddaughter sitting at her kitchen table. "This is nice." She looked at the clock on the stove. "Oh, my, it's early. Well, the good news is you have plenty of time for biscuits and gravy for breakfast."

Arthur patted Jobie's hand. "Good thing neither one of us has to worry about our waistlines."

Jobie got up from the table and poured her grandfather and herself another cup of coffee. "I will if I stay here very long. I'm not sixteen anymore."

***

Jobie sat at the kitchen table with her guitar, fingering random chords and glancing at the phone on the wall every few minutes, as though she could will it to ring. Deedee was late calling, and Lily and Arthur had gone to bed already. Jobie suspected they wanted to give her some privacy for the call.

The phone rang, and Jobie picked up before the first ring died away. Did that seem too anxious? "Deedee?"

"It's me. Am I late calling? Believe it or not, I'm still at the studio."

Jobie slumped in her chair, feeling let down that she might still have to compete for Deedee's attention.

Deedee blew out a long breath. "It's good to relax a minute and talk to you. I'm in some network suit's dark office while he's home cozy in bed. I'm having to learn a lot about studio politics, not exactly my strong point. Again, thank goodness for Kate."

"Yes, thank goodness," Jobie said.

"Tell me what you're struggling with, and before we ring off, I have something to talk to you about, too."

Jobie wanted to let Deedee know that she was considering taking a break from her music and moving back to Jasper for a while. She wanted Deedee's advice, but her more important goal was to probe whether Deedee felt as she did about getting closer. She wanted to find a way they could spend more time together, but she was reluctant to press Deedee with all she had on her mind. She dodged the question. "You go first."

"I want you to come over and appear on my show, not just a one-off appearance, but to be a regular. I have to give credit where it's due. It was Kate's idea."

"Kate's idea?"

"Yes, she thinks your music and your look are a nice counterpoint to me and to the whoop-de-do production numbers that the BBC thinks are necessary, with all the dancers and glittery costumes. That's part of the politics I was talking about. Even though I'm supposed to have complete artistic control, some of them still want to put their tuppence in."

Jobie pictured the American variety shows starring singers and comedians that made the jump from radio and movies to the relatively new medium of TV. It sounded as though the BBC had in mind copying that successful format. "If I appeared on your show, would I be expected to dance and wear glittery costumes?"

"No." Deedee laughed. "That's the point. We want a different kind of show, with more variety and appealing to a younger audience. Your music and your look are straightforward and pure." Her voice became low and insinuating. "They don't know what I do about your impure side. Mmm, in fact, I'm caressing the impure parts right now."

Jobie felt a buzz in the pit of her stomach. "I miss you so much."

"I miss you, too, and your being on the show has definite side benefits. We can be together all the time."

That was what Jobie wanted to hear. Still, she felt a prick of concern about making the decision to go to London. When Deedee said they would be together all the time, she meant the time she could spare from developing and starring in a new TV show. Deedee's perfectionist nature and her determination to control every aspect wouldn't leave much time for a new girlfriend. And she said their being together would be a side benefit. She meant well, but Jobie suspected that their relationship might prove to come in second to Deedee's work and her ambition. And Jobie was suspicious of Kate having the best interests of their relationship at heart.

"Can I think it over?"

There was a pause on Deedee's end, and when she answered, Jobie could hear surprise after the hesitation. "Well, of course. I know it would be a big decision."

Jobie rushed on. "It's just that my recording contract is over soon, and I'm thinking of giving up music for a while. That's the quandary I wanted to talk to you about. I'm thinking of working full time on my painting, until I can get enough work together to show to a gallery. If I don't try, I'll always wonder whether I'd have been good enough. What do you think?"

"You're asking me for advice? I'm not sure I can be objective. I'm disappointed that it would mean you won't come over for the show. It seems like such a perfect way for us to be together. Let me try to put that aside for a minute. I don't know the art world. What I've seen of your drawings are impressive, but giving up music? This practical question may surprise you, coming from me, but how would you support yourself?"

"I'll sublease my apartment and come back to Jasper to stay with Mama and Papa for a while, six months or so. They're totally for it."

"I know they'd be overjoyed with that, but are you sure they're in any better position to give you objective advice than I am? They love you, too." *They love you, too.* Deedee tossed that off almost too casually. "Not to pressure you, but Kate's laying out the shows now for the whole season, guest stars and so on, so we need to decide."

"Let me think about it overnight, okay?"

"Of course. I wish I was there to convince you in person."

"In a way, so do I, but it's a decision I need to make and live with the consequences."

They said their goodbyes and Jobie hung up. She turned off the kitchen light and pushed through the screen door onto the back porch. The moon was full, and even though Jasper was too small a town to have streetlights, she could see past the smokehouse that Papa promised to remodel for her studio. From one of the tall pine trees marking the edge of their property, an owl hooted the question, *Who? Who?*

"It's only me."

The phone in the kitchen jangled.

"Jobie, it's me again. Kate has a grand idea. While you're deciding, why don't you come over and do a guest appearance. No commitment beyond that. You can see what it's like, and maybe that will help you make up your mind."

"I suppose I could do that." Jobie slid down the wall to sit cross-legged on the cool linoleum. "Why not?"

"Perfect. Where will you fly from? We'll have a ticket waiting at the airport. How soon can you come? I'll put Kate on the line to work out all the details. Jobie?"

"Yes."

"Come as soon as you can."

Chapter Twenty-eight

DEEDEE'S BRAND-NEW RED Buick convertible sped down the two-lane country road in the Cotswolds north of London. Deedee looked over at Jobie and patted her leg. "Relax. You're sitting on the edge of your seat and gripping the dash for dear life. How are we going to have the nice Sunday drive I promised when you're so uptight? It's my only day off. I want us to enjoy it."

"Sorry."

"What are you so nervous about right this minute?"

"Let me see." Jobie let go of the dashboard to tick off the reasons on her fingers. "The fact that we're driving on the wrong side of the road, which I'll never get used to by the way, and this American car is built for driving on the right side of the road. The fact that you are practically blind and refuse to wear glasses to drive. And finally, that you drive too fast."

"Fair enough. Do you want to drive?"

"No. That's the only thing that could make it worse."

"Good. We're almost there anyway."

"Where are we going?"

"It's a surprise."

They came to a T intersection and turned right onto an even narrower road. Stone buildings lined both sides. Deedee pointed out an ancient-looking sign that said, *Chipping Campden.* "Welcome to Chipping Campden, the jewel of the Cotswolds," Deedee said.

They drove into the village. The buildings of honey-colored limestone crowded close together on both sides of High Street. "See that building right there?" Deedee pointed toward an arched pavilion of the same limestone. "It was built in 1627 for the wool merchants to show their wares." She drove slowly through the village toward a gothic church tower that rose above the trees at the edge of town. She stopped the car in front of a lane across from the church and pulled a piece of paper from her jeans pocket. "This is it." She turned into the lane and parked in front of a hedge-and-stone garden wall enclosing a thatch-roofed cottage made of the same stone as the buildings they had passed along the main shopping street. "We're here." Deedee stepped out of the car, went around to Jobie's side, took her hand, and helped her out. "What do you think?"

"It's beautiful. Whose is it?"

"It's mine."

"What?" Jobie leaned against the car and looked from Deedee's face to the cottage.

"I bought it. Kate found it for me. I've been thinking that I need a place to get away from London. The flat in the city close to the studio is good, but I need tranquility sometimes. Kate says it has a perfect little studio in the back with great light for painting." Deedee started toward the gate. She turned back when Jobie didn't move from leaning against the car. "What?"

Jobie shook her head. "Sounds like you and Kate have it all worked out."

"Jobie, are you going to spoil the surprise? I thought you'd be happy for me."

"A getaway sounds fine, in theory, but how will you ever take time to be here?" Jobie couldn't get a picture of Deedee relaxing in a cottage away from the frantic hustle of her life in London.

"Just come and look. Keep your mind open." Deedee pulled a key out of her pocket.

Jobie pushed herself away from the car and followed Deedee through the gate in the low stone wall.

The front door swung into a small living area with a beamed ceiling. A stone fireplace took up one wall. An archway led to the kitchen furnished with a spotless antique stove and refrigerator. The kitchen fireplace was big enough to stand up in. A narrow, winding staircase led to two bedrooms under the eaves with a newly remodeled bathroom between.

Deedee looked around the empty rooms. "I'll have to furnish the cottage. I expect there are some wonderful pieces to be had right here in the village." She embraced Jobie and kissed her and nuzzled her neck. "The first thing I'll buy is a bed. One of those big carved ones with the canopy on top that you have to climb up steps to get into. I've always fancied one of those. I'll bet it would make you feel as randy as Queen Anne."

Jobie laughed and kissed Deedee back. "How will you get a bed like that up those narrow stairs to the bedroom?"

"You're always so practical. I find practical very sexy." They went back down the stairs. Deedee opened a back door leading out to the garden. "Let's look out back."

There was a small studio, with walls of glass all around that had clearly been added in modern times. Jobie stood in the middle of the studio and pictured where an easel should sit to take advantage of the sunlight streaming through the glass.

"Wait till you see the rest." She took Jobie's hand and led her back through the cottage, out the gate, and across the lane to a stone marker with a brass plate that read, *Cotswold Way, The Beginning and the End.*

"Chipping Campden is the northern end of a hundred-mile-long hiking trail that finishes in Bath to the south. Come on." She led Jobie to a rock fence with a stile and a hand-painted wooden arrow that said, *Cotswold Way.* They climbed over the fence and followed the narrow path up a steep, grassy hill dotted with yellow wildflowers. Black-faced sheep raised their heads to check whether they should pay attention to these two-legged intruders. Finding them harmless, they went back to their grazing.

At the top of the hill, Jobie and Deedee stopped to catch their breaths and gaze over the valley to the north. There were fields laid out in irregular squares like a crazy patchwork quilt.

"Look around." Deedee made a sweeping motion that took in the village to the south and the valley in front of them. "Painters come here from all over the world." Deedee put up her hands. "I know, I know. I'm not pressuring. Just saying if you were to stay here in England for a while, this is a great place to work on paintings for a show in New York, or maybe even London."

"So, I'd be the girlfriend installed in an idyllic cottage who you visit whenever you can run away from London for a few days?"

"Jobie, it's not like that. You've said you're thinking of giving up your music to focus on painting. If you do, this is one of the world-class places to paint. And at the same time, it's a great getaway for me."

"I still have my apartment in New York to think about."

"Keep it. You have a lease, right? I can afford to pay for it for a while, now that I have the show. Who knows when we might need to go to New York?"

"That's very generous, but let's take one step at a time and get this guest appearance on your show behind us."

"You make it sound as though you're swallowing castor oil. Aren't you even a little looking forward to the show?"

"It's nothing against the show. If I'm going to paint, I'm anxious to get on with it. I think the cottage is lovely. The studio would be perfect for my work. Let's see how the show goes, and at the risk of being practical again, shouldn't we get back on the road to the city? I can't imagine that you drive any better in the dark."

"You're right, but first tell me that you're excited about my cottage, and that it will make you think more favorably of staying. We can work out the rest."

"We'll see."

"I'll take that for now."

Chapter Twenty-nine

THE SMELL OF FRESH-SAWN pine lumber dominated the usual scent of oil paint and turpentine in Jobie's small studio. She pounded in the last nail of a shipping frame around a large canvas. The frame would stabilize the picture and the freight office in London would pack it in straw, along with two dozen others, for a freighter trip across the Atlantic to the gallery in Soho.

Jobie propped the painting against the wall and stood back with her hands on her hips and sighed. "That's done, Scout, though I have to say you weren't much help, except for moral support." Scout, a chocolate Labrador, was napping in a sunny spot, his head on his paws. He opened his eyes at the familiar sound of his name but didn't budge.

"No, no, don't rouse yourself. Moral support is important, too." She bent to scratch his ears, the way he liked. He moaned a thank you.

The phone in the cottage jangled, making her jump. "Damn! I have to get an extension out here." She wiped her hands on a paint-stained rag as she ran inside. "Hello."

"Jobie, it's me. I miss you. What are you doing?"

"Scout and I are celebrating six months of work completed. We're toasting each other, which is quite a trick on Scout's part, since he doesn't have opposable thumbs."

Deedee giggled.

"We're preparing my paintings to be packed for shipping. When are you getting on the road?"

Deedee hesitated. "That's what I called to tell you. I'm not going to be able to come out tonight."

"Oh." Jobie felt disappointment harden like a stone in her chest. It wasn't that the change in plans was unusual. More often than not, Deedee backed out on her promise to drive to Chipping Campden for a couple of days, or even a few hours, together. When Jobie agreed six months ago to come to live in the cottage and paint, she told herself that she would be clear-eyed about her expectations. Still, it hurt.

Deedee rushed on. "We're having a devil of a time with Judy

Garland. The entire London Palladium Orchestra is here in the studio just standing around. She won't come out of her dressing room. Kate's down there right now trying to talk to her."

"You've been so excited about having her on as a guest."

"I know. We've all been, including the network. We'll pull it together. It's not as though Garland hasn't performed these songs a million times. From what I've heard, she always comes through in the end. Maybe I'm whistling past the graveyard thinking she'll come through again this time."

"I hope you're not being too optimistic."

"So do I, but the fact is we have to get it together. We've been touting this show for days. We hope to get just the bump we need in the ratings. Plus, I think our voices would be incredible together, and from the looks of her, this might be the only time I can find out."

Jobie heard Kate's voice in the background. "Just a minute, Jobie." Deedee went away from the phone, and Jobie could hear the frustration in her muffled responses. "We'll have to rehearse it without her. Get one of the singers to stand in for blocking the shots." Deedee came back on the line. "I've got to go."

"Do you want us to come there?" Scout had followed her into the cottage, and he was standing by her knee, staring intently at her face. "Scout says he and I could at least lend moral support. He's good at that, you know."

"No, no. We'll work through it. I have to go. I'll call you after the show."

They said their goodbyes, and Jobie sat holding the dead receiver in her hand. She couldn't shake the feeling of disappointment that Deedee's plans were changed. Her emotions warred with each other as she thought about the benefits that Deedee had given her weighed against the dissatisfaction she was feeling. Deedee provided the charming cottage in a beautiful setting and supported Jobie's time to create paintings for a show. On the other hand, she felt lonely and off-balance in their relationship.

She shook her head to clear her thoughts and looked around the cottage. "Let's walk down to Badgers Hall for some tea, Scout." She found his leash, grabbed her sketchbook and a box of charcoals, and walked the short block to High Street, turning right toward the center of town. Scout seemed glad to stretch his legs. He pranced along by her side, glancing up at her every so often. Jobie reached down to pet his head. "This is better than sitting around feeling sorry for ourselves, right?"

They passed St. James' Church, and then the gates to Old Campden House. Jobie detoured up the pea gravel path and paused to peek through the padlocked gate. The great and imposing residence of a wealthy wool merchant was burned 350 years ago, during the English Civil War. What was left were two charming banqueting halls and a gatehouse.

Past the estate walls, the sixteenth-century village almshouse was next. She crossed the street to get a better view, only at the last second remembering to look to the right instead of the left for oncoming traffic. "I'll never get used to it, Scout." She sat down cross-legged on the grass. The pale honeycomb color of the stones of the almshouse looked pleasantly aged by the gentle washing of hundreds of years of rain. "Can you wait a minute and let me get a sketch of the almshouse? I haven't drawn it in exactly this light before."

Scout settled in patiently by her side. Jobie took out her charcoals and began to sketch the building, but she felt too distracted to focus on her drawing. A picture kept intruding of Deedee and Kate trying to deal with the confusion in Studio 2 at BBC, fifty or sixty orchestra members, backup singers, and dancers milling around waiting for Judy Garland to finally make an appearance for a run-through of her numbers.

"We could skip tea and drive into London. Maybe we could help if we were there. Why not? My paintings are ready to go to the freight office, so I could get that done, too. If we leave now, we'll be there before they close." Jobie packed her charcoals and headed back to the cottage. She threw some clothes in a bag, packed food, chew toys, a blanket, and a bed for Scout, and loaded them, along with the paintings, in the bright yellow Land Rover Deedee had surprised her with on her birthday.

Jobie made it to the freight office near Hyde Park in London just in time before closing. She got a nice compliment on her paintings from the shipping clerk. He was born and raised in the Cotswolds. He said that her paintings captured the feel of the countryside, and he especially loved the portraits of Chipping Campden citizens. He said the works took him back to his childhood. Jobie interpreted this as a good omen that the paintings would make it safely all the way to the gallery in Greenwich Village, and that her show would be a success.

Jobie turned her car into the boulevard that bisected the green expanse of Hyde Park. She parked and hooked up Scout's leash to give him some exercise after being cooped up in the car. She let him off the leash to chase tennis balls. She was always careful to bring three balls. Scout didn't exactly get the concept of fetch. He thought it was a lot more fun to ignore the retriever part of his breed name and instead play catch and keep-away. His mouth could hold two balls, but not three. He had to drop one to catch the next, which kept the game going. Who was manipulating who?

After a good long romp, Jobie loaded Scout back in the car. She carefully navigated through the busy rush-hour streets. After six months, she still silently repeated the mantra, *left side, left side, left side*. She turned into Westbourne Terrace where Deedee kept the small apartment, even though she could easily afford a more fashionable neighborhood now. Jobie remembered the first time she had come to a spaghetti dinner at Deedee's place, after the *Thank Your Lucky Stars* TV show. She began to fall in love with Deedee that night.

Scout started whining when she parked the Land Rover across the street from the Regency-style row houses. Jobie laughed. "I know you love her, buddy. I do, too." Scout more than loved Deedee—he was in love with her. Their time together was rare enough that it always seemed special. Jobie and Scout crossed the wide boulevard, busy with traffic in the gathering gloom.

She climbed the front steps and held the end of Scout's leather leash between her teeth as she unlocked the front door. If he took off after a squirrel, which had been known to happen, they'd make quite a picture stumbling down the street. She located the key, opened the door, and almost ran into Marilyn just stepping off the stairs from her second-floor apartment.

Marilyn stopped in her tracks. "Jobie. You're here."

"Yes, Deedee couldn't come to the cottage, plus I have some business here in the city, so we came to her."

Marilyn reached down to scratch Scout's ear. "I see you have. Did Deedee know you were coming?" She glanced behind her toward Deedee's door at the end of the hallway.

"No, it's a surprise. She's still at the studio, I suppose. Did they get Judy Garland squared away? Did you finish your numbers already?"

"Yes, they got Miss Garland squared away. It was amazing to see her and Deedee together. They did a duet of 'The Man That Got Away.' It was incredible."

"Deedee thought their voices together might be something special. Well..." Jobie took a step toward Deedee's apartment.

"How have you been, Jobie? I'm sorry things didn't work out for you with the show."

"Don't be. It's just not for me. I did the one guest appearance. That was enough to tell me that it's not my cup of tea. Did she tell you that I got a gallery exhibition in New York for my paintings? It's in six weeks. I just shipped my paintings off."

"Yes, she told us about your exhibit. She's very proud of you. Still, Deedee could use more of your steadying influence at the studio."

"She's got Kate for that."

Marilyn cleared her throat and glanced again toward Deedee's door. "Kate's certainly important to the show, but I can always tell when Deedee's been able to spend time with you in the country. She comes back with her head on straighter. Of course, things don't take long to get tense again. She wants the show to be perfect. She feels so much responsibility for the success of *DEEDEE!* and for all of us."

Jobie glanced outside the front door that was standing open. A few feet away on the sidewalk a steady stream of people hurried back and forth. She felt uncomfortable talking out in the open with Marilyn about Deedee, and Scout was pacing and whining.

"Are you in a hurry, or do you want to come in for some tea or wine or something? I'll just get Scout settled in the apartment and go back to the car for our things."

Marilyn hesitated. "I..." She shook her head and shrugged. "I have to go." She hugged Jobie. "Deedee really cares about you." She gave Scout another pet. "Goodbye, Jobie." She headed out the door.

Jobie watched her practically run down the sidewalk without a backward look. "That was strange." She steered Scout through the hallway and unlocked the apartment door. Scout butted the door open and bounded into the room, barking joyously and jumping on Deedee with his front paws reaching almost to her shoulders.

Things after that seemed to happen in flashes of images like a sped-up slideshow without sound: the comically shocked look on Deedee's face; Kate sitting up in the rumpled bed and awkwardly grabbing the edge of the sheet to cover her naked breasts; Deedee catching Scout's front paws, lowering him gently to the floor, and reaching her hand out to Jobie.

Jobie threw the keys as hard as she could, hitting Deedee full in the chest. Then she was running down the hallway, out the front door and across the street to her car, desperate to get away before Deedee caught up with her. As she got to the car, it dawned on her what a stupid thing she'd done, throwing the keys. Deedee came running into the street, barefoot and in a robe. "Jobie, wait!"

"Give me the keys."

"Jobie, where are you going? Let me talk to you. Just wait a minute. Kate's gone. Let's just sit down for a minute. I didn't know you were coming."

"That's what you have to say? You didn't know I was coming?" Jobie shook her head and held out her hand. "Give me the keys. I see you have them. Give them to me." The look on her face and the tone of her voice must have told Deedee that pleading was useless. She handed over the keys.

Jobie lurched away from the curb and looked in the rearview mirror. Deedee was standing in the middle of the boulevard looking after the car, her arms dangling at her sides. Jobie stomped on the brake and threw the car in reverse. The tires squealed as she backed up next to Deedee. "And you goddam well better take care of Scout!"

She threw the car into drive again and sped away. Jobie stared straight ahead, her eyes hot and dry as she focused on navigating through the heavy traffic toward Heathrow. At last, she began to see planes landing and taking off and then the control tower rising above the trees. She turned the Land Rover into a parking structure, wound up to the top level, and parked as far away from other cars as possible. She rested her forehead against the steering wheel as the images of Deedee and Kate in the apartment replayed over and over unbidden across her mind. She felt she was moving into a hailstorm of emotion and pain, with a rising sense of panic. She had no idea how big the storm would grow and whether the hurt and humiliation would overwhelm her.

How could she do it? And how could I let this happen? How could I make such a mistake? What Jobie wanted at this moment was to stop torturing herself with these questions and just get away. She willed her hands to stop shaking long enough to retrieve her small suitcase from under Scout's blanket in the back seat. She picked up the blanket and sobbed into it until she could get control of herself. She hid the key on top of the front tire on the driver's side and rushed into the international terminal.

***

During the long ride from Newark airport, through the Lincoln Tunnel, into Manhattan, and finally to her apartment across from Washington Square, Jobie felt relieved that the cabbie was silent instead of chatty and left her alone with her thoughts.

The phone was ringing when Jobie unlocked the front door. She rushed to answer it, then hesitated, her hand hovering over the receiver. She checked her watch again. "One o'clock in the morning." If it was her grandparents, they might be calling because Deedee had contacted them looking for her. They'd be up in the middle of the night and worried. If it was Deedee, Jobie was sure she wasn't ready to talk to her. She guessed the odds were fifty-fifty.

She raised the receiver. "Hello."

"Jobie, it's Mama and Papa. Are you all right? Deedee called here looking for you."

She was relieved for a moment but heard the concern in her grandmother's voice and silently swore at Deedee for bothering them. "Yes, I just got off the plane from London, so I may not make much sense, but I am all right. I'm in New York. But you know that because you called me."

Her nervous laugh turned into a sob, and she couldn't go on. She heard her grandmother say, "Arthur," and her grandfather came on the line.

"Go to bed and get some sleep, honey. We're coming up there."

Jobie hung up the phone and dropped her head in her hands. It rang again. "Papa?"

"Jobie, it's me." It was Deedee.

"I can't talk to you right now."

"I've been up all night trying to find you. You have to talk to me on the phone or I'm coming there."

"Don't do that."

"We have to talk, Jobie."

"Don't call me again. I can't talk to you yet. I'll call you in a few days."

"Promise?"

"Yes."

Chapter Thirty

LILY AND JOBIE SAT on her front steps facing the park that was crowded with people. It was Saturday morning and the first truly warm day of spring. Lily tilted her head back and let the sun warm her face. "I smell blooming trees, just like in Tennessee. I didn't know New York had blooming trees."

Jobie put her hand on Lily's on the cement step beside her. "I appreciate you and Papa driving all the way up here, but—"

"Honey, that's the last time I want to hear you apologize for letting us help you if we can. We had a nice drive up here. Stopped for the night in Virginia halfway, and now Papa's getting to sleep late, which he never does at home. He has some notion that you might come back with us, but I know you won't now you've got your gallery show, will you?"

"No. My life is here now. I'm just trying to make sure to not mess it up. I feel so lucky being raised in Jasper and having you and Papa. Sometimes I think about the three of us together and how much simpler it seemed in Tennessee, but I have to make my own way here now."

"You won't forget us, will you?"

"No, never."

Lily took a tissue from her pocket and dabbed at her eyes. "That's enough of that. You've reminded me that I brought you a present." She went into the apartment and came back carrying an oddly shaped package wrapped in Christmas paper. "Excuse the paper. It was all I had handy when we left home so fast."

Jobie tore open the wrapping and gasped. "Mama, this is your cornbread skillet."

"Now you can make good cornbread, and every time you do, you'll think of us."

"But what about Papa's cornbread?"

"He'll live. It was his idea. I'm sure he knew all along you wouldn't come home with us." Lily took the tissue out of her pocket again and wiped Jobie's eyes. "Now, tell me what's going on with this girlfriend of yours?"

"I'm not sure I can put it all in words. She betrayed me, and I'm just so hurt by her and angry with myself." Jobie told her grandmother about finding Deedee with Kate in her London apartment.

"Why in the world are you angry with yourself?"

"I should have seen it coming. I knew from the very first that Deedee had a history with Kate and that Kate still had feelings for her, and they worked closely together every day. Kate is so important to her career. I know that. I even respect it, but Deedee doesn't make a boundary between her career and her personal life. I was alone out in the Cotswolds immersed in my painting, but only because she was so busy. Deedee found it harder and harder to get away so we could be together."

Lily hugged Jobie. "You're being too hard on yourself. You said Deedee betrayed you."

"Well, that's the thing. A commitment to be exclusive is important to me, but I didn't press Deedee for that. Maybe I was afraid of what her answer would be. I can't claim I got a clear promise from her."

Down the street, they heard a rumbling sound, and as it grew louder, they saw a man pushing a grand piano on wheels through the memorial archway into the square. They watched him park the piano in front of the fountain, prop open the soundboard cover, set out his tip jar, and salt it with a few bills.

Lily looked at Jobie with her mouth open.

"You're in Greenwich Village, New York City."

Lily nodded and laughed. "I almost came to New York City one time, long ago. I finally got here."

"Was that when you were a dancer?"

"Right after." Lily glanced at Jobie. "I've never told you the whole story about Jobyna Jones, but I think now might be the time. I've always wanted to be careful not to hurt your Papa, and like the situation with you and Deedee, I'm not sure I can explain it all, even this long a time afterward." She looked over her shoulder at the front door. "Let's go sit in the park."

They found an empty bench facing Jobie's apartment so they could see Arthur if he woke up and came looking for them. Across the square, the pianist put on a black top hat and a tailcoat that he took from his duffel bag, bowed solemnly to an imaginary audience, sat at the piano, and began playing the familiar movement of a Rachmaninoff concerto.

Jobie prompted her grandmother to tell the story she had started. "What about Jobyna?"

"I was seventeen years old. I thought if I could just get away from the farm in Chattanooga there was some big adventure waiting out there with me as the main character. Our cousin Ruth got me a tryout as a dancer with a traveling show. That was the first time I saw Jobyna Jones. Before long, I thought I was finally going to live out my big adventure, and now there were two main characters: Jobyna Jones, Empress of the Blues, and me."

"Wait, you were in a relationship with Jobyna Jones?"

"I loved her. She cared for me, I know, and I think if things had gone different, we would have been together, at least for a time. She was going to send for me to come to New York. She said she'd get a house for us. But Jobyna lived a complicated life. She had her career and the business that went along with it."

"Like Deedee does. That hasn't changed in the forty years gone by."

"And she had other people in her life."

"Other women?"

Lily nodded.

"And didn't she have a husband? Wasn't he the one who shot her?"

"Little T wasn't her husband, but he was her man and tried to be her business manager, too, but he wasn't very good at it. She depended on him, though."

"Was she going to give up the other people in her life for you?"

"We never got that far. Like you, I never asked her for that. Little T never would have given her up."

"He might have shot you, too."

"I worried some about that, I knew he had a gun. But I would have gone to her anyway." Her eyes took on an unfocused and faraway look. "I can still hear her voice sometimes when things are quiet."

"What about Papa?" *And what about me?* Jobie felt a vague jealousy imagining the depth of her grandmother's feelings for this faraway figure that meant so much to seventeen-year-old Lily.

"He came along right about when I lost her. It took me time to get over Jobyna and I had to learn to love him. But he was patient, and I did learn to love him. He gave me the strength to get over her. I wouldn't change any of that. It's how we got you."

Jobie hugged her grandmother. "I wanted to hear that."

The pianist started a Scott Joplin ragtime tune. "Do you think I should try to go on with Deedee?"

"Oh, Jobie, you can't ask me that. Right now, I want to whip her for hurting you. You have to listen to the voice inside you. But if you do decide to go on with her, you have to tell her what you want."

"I want what you and Papa have."

"Then you must tell her that." She pointed across the square. "Here he comes now."

Arthur raised his eyebrows and made a comic face as he passed the piano. He plopped down on the bench between the two of them. "We are not in Tennessee anymore, Lily."

"No, Papa, we most surely are not. Jobie says we can walk from here to the Empire State Building. Would you like that?"

"Let's go." He offered an arm to each of them and they headed north up Fifth Avenue.

Chapter Thirty-one

JOBIE CLIMBED OFF THE step stool and stood back to gauge whether the draperies on her front window were hanging straight after she had taken them down and washed them. She glanced at the vacuum cleaner waiting in the middle of the living room floor, and then checked her watch. Five o'clock in the morning. She was sure her neighbors wouldn't appreciate being awakened before dawn on Sunday morning by the machine's loud whine.

When her grandparents went back to Tennessee, she lost a handy distraction from the situation with Deedee. Then yesterday, the letter from Deedee arrived. She flopped from back to front and right to left through the long hours last night, unable to turn off her brain and surrender to sleep. Finally, she gave up, got out of bed, and began deep cleaning her apartment.

She stood in the middle of the living room and turned in a circle, searching for something quiet to keep herself occupied. The lavender pages of Deedee's letter, lying on the coffee table, snagged her attention. She sat on the sofa and picked it up to read it again for the ninth or tenth time.

Dear Jobie,

I'm doing what you said. I'm not calling you, and I'm trusting you'll keep your promise to call me. I do need to tell you some things. The other day was the first time anything like that has happened since you and I have been together. I told you the truth about needing to stay in London because of the show. I had no intention of lying to you.

You know firsthand how much pressure I've been under the last few months, trying to make DEEDEE! *a success. Getting through the first season, with the network breathing down our necks, is critically important for the future. I don't mean just my future, I mean ours— yours and mine. Once we get through the first season, everyone will relax a little. The sponsors get locked in, we're able to book better guests, and I have the leeway to do the kind of show I want to.*

That week was the worst so far. We were counting on Judy Garland's guest appearance to boost our ratings—which it did, by the way. She was a mess, but as we hoped she came through once the little red light on the TV camera came on. It was like she became a different person. I think she's a genius, and maybe all geniuses are difficult. It was a real lesson for me.

Way back when I first came to your apartment in New York, you asked me about Kate's feelings for me, and I think I was honest with you about that. She feels terrible about the other day, by the way. She would never want to deliberately hurt you. Anyway, I couldn't have done all this without her. From the time she first encouraged me to go solo to now, she has taken care of me. As I told you then, the physical part between us was short-lived and has been over for a long time. That is true. Last week was a fluke.

I'm so proud of you going after your dream of pursuing your art and getting your show in the gallery there in SoHo. You must be working hard on it by now. I've always felt you support me, too. That's a good thing about us.

I only hope you will consider all this and call me so we can talk. Scout is lying with his chin on my feet, watching me write this letter and sending his love to you. I am, too.

Deedee

She checked her watch again. There was a good chance that Deedee would still be sleeping, but she picked up the phone and dialed the apartment in London before she could change her mind.

Deedee picked up right away and sounded alert, her tone expectant, as though she knew it was Jobie. "Hello?"

Jobie's pulse quickened at the sound of her voice. "It's me."

"Yes. I'm glad you called me."

"How was the show last night?"

"It was good. Tom Jones was on. Did you know that he stuffs his pants with socks?"

"Oh, no." Jobie scrubbed her hand across her eyes. "I didn't need that visual."

Deedee chuckled. "How is your gallery show going?"

"It opens in three weeks. Right now, we're doing publicity. They're casting me as a musician who paints instead of an artist. Not my favorite approach, but I guess it's to be expected for my first show. The gallery owner is remarkable. You'd like her."

"Attractive?"

"That's where your mind goes immediately? Yes, she's attractive, but that's not what's remarkable about her. She had a tiny gallery on the Upper East Side. The collection was well-reviewed, but a critic wrote in the newspaper that the owner, Paula Stone, was a 'dumb girl.' Instead of being devastated, which I might have been, she moved to a less snooty neighborhood. Mine will be her first show in Soho. She's taking a chance on me."

"I predict a hugely successful opening. Then you can come back to me in triumph."

Jobie could practically see and feel the other shoe dropping. "Deedee—"

"You got my letter, didn't you? You do believe that I didn't plan it."

"Yes, I believe you, but you didn't promise that it will never happen again. Might it, with Kate or someone else?"

"Well...I didn't lie before, so I won't start now. I can promise the best intentions, but who really knows. I'm not even sure it's realistic to expect to always find everything you need in one person. Sometimes I need escape with someone who doesn't see all my failings."

"I'm not expecting that we would be perfect for each other all the time, but that we would always be trying, not willing to just find somebody else, even in the short term."

"That sounds like a lot of work."

"I think it is." Jobie began to cry as the full weight of the reality of giving up Deedee hit her.

"Don't cry." Deedee blew out a breath of frustration. "We shouldn't be deciding things like this on the phone. Will you come back after your opening?"

"I don't think so."

"I wish you wouldn't do this, Jobie. Can I come to New York?"

"No. Let's leave it here."

"I can't just leave it. I don't want to lose you in my life, Jobie. Can I call you? I'm going to call you."

Jobie wiped her eyes. "Wait a while."

Chapter Thirty-two

THE PAULA STONE GALLERY was in the middle of a block of one-story structures with cast-iron facades dating back to the middle of the nineteenth century. The buildings were originally garment factories and the strong exoskeletons of iron allowed large, wide-open spaces that were perfect repurposed for displaying art. The gallery's white walls were brightly lit for Jobie's opening. The original hardwood floors gleamed with reflected light.

Jobie stood in the middle of the gallery, packed with a crowd milling among the two dozen works, the bar, and the hors d'oeuvres table. Most of the paintings already had red dots on the small title plates next to each work, indicating they had been spoken for. Paula Stone came to Jobie's side. She was small, no bigger than a twelve-year-old girl, but the alert look in her eyes, which seemed to take in everything going on in the large room, signaled her shrewd business instincts. She leaned to whisper in Jobie's ear. "You see. I told you we had great buzz. I'm so glad that bastard from the *Herald Tribune* is here to see it. I just overheard him bragging that he discovered you."

She took Jobie's empty champagne glass and handed her a full one. "We just sold my favorite, *The Almshouse.*"

"Who bought it?"

"That's the best part. Amy Austin bought it."

"Amy Austin...Andy Warhol's friend?"

"Yes. Her buying the painting will make the papers. Great publicity. Do you know her?"

"No."

Paula stood on tiptoes to look over the crowd and gestured with the empty champagne glass toward a group of women near the bar. "The thin one with short blond hair and chandelier earrings."

Standing next to Austin and in deep conversation with her, was a woman with unmistakable long, straight, silky-silver hair. It was Clair. As Jobie watched, Austin put her hand on Clair's forearm in a gesture that seemed so familiar and intimate that it made Jobie feel she was eavesdropping. She averted her eyes.

"Don't you want to go over and thank her?"

"Don't bother her right now. I'll circle around to them later."

"Fine. You should be circulating. Patrons love that. They want to rub elbows with the talent. That sells."

Jobie moved purposefully from painting to painting, sipping champagne and chatting with small groups about Chipping Campden, the thatched-roofed cottages, seventeenth-century stone buildings, and the villagers. Paula was right; the potential buyers really seemed to enjoy meeting her and knowing the background of the works.

"Jobie." Clair took her arm and pulled her to the side and hugged her. "I've missed you. This is wonderful. I'm proud of you."

"I saw you across the room, and I was so glad, and surprised." Jobie looked around. "Where are your friends? Amy Austin bought one of my paintings."

"Yes, I know she did."

"I wanted to meet her and thank her."

"They went on to the next party. They don't light for long in any one place. So, what about you? From the subjects of your paintings, I take it you've been in England all this time."

"Yes. I've been back in New York for about a month."

"To get ready for the show?"

"That...and I've moved back for good."

"Oh."

"Yes. 'Different expectations about the relationship.' Isn't that what you called your long-distance love experience the night we had dinner at the Coach House?"

Clair looked around at the thinning crowd. "It's hard to talk here. Do you need to stay, or could we go across the street for a coffee?"

It had rained at some point during the evening, making the cobblestones slick. "Careful," Clair said, and she took Jobie's hand as they crossed the street. Jobie held on even after they were safely across, enjoying the warmth of Clair's skin against her own.

Clair glanced at her. "What's the joke? Why are you smiling?"

"Have you ever noticed that sometimes when you hold a person's hand, it feels like a natural fit, and with some people you have to learn how to hold hands with them?"

"Am I the first kind?"

"Yes."

"Good." A little smile played around Clair's mouth.

They found a table inside by the front window. When they had settled with their coffee, Clair said, "Now, what about Deedee?"

"A long story, but I'll just say we agreed to call it off and to stay friends. I respect her talent so much. Her BBC show is a big hit. And she supported my painting when it was really important. She's coming over this summer to be in a musical on Broadway." She heard the pride in her own voice telling Clair about Deedee's success.

Clair raised her eyebrows. "Are you sure it's over?"

"Oh, it's over. Don't ask me to go into the gory details. Maybe I will someday, if you want to hear them." Jobie stared into her coffee and smoothed the cowlick at her hairline. "And you?"

"We're still doing college tours and playing clubs around the US and Canada, and our albums are selling okay. I'm not going to record a solo album. It's just not me. As long as the boys want to go on, I guess we'll be the Three Musketeers."

"What about personal?"

"Oh, I don't have much time for that."

"Come on, what about Amy Austin? She seems to be totally into you."

"She's a friend. Fun, smart, interesting, and incredibly generous. When I admired your painting tonight, she bought it for me."

"She bought it for you?"

"Yes, I love *The Almshouse.* You're really good."

"Do you remember when we had dinner at the Coach House you promised to sit for me? Will you?"

"Of course."

"So, you were saying that Amy's just a friend."

"She told me once that she feels like her whole life is a television show. I'm an actor in the show right now, but not anything beyond that. It's not my kind of life anyway."

"It sounds like we are both blessed with interesting, successful, and generous friends." Jobie took Clair's hand again. "It seems you and I keep flirting with something more than that. Does it seem that way to you?"

"Yes, it does."

"Isn't it time to do something about that?"

"We could discuss it further over cornbread at the Coach House."

"Sounds like a plan. Or we could go to my apartment, and I can make us cornbread."

"Sounds like a better plan."

EPILOGUE

2004

SONDRA OPENED THE DOOR and stuck her head in. "Miz Lily, are you awake?"

"Yes, honey. Just resting my eyes."

Sondra came into the room and held out a small plate with a cupcake and a candle burning on the top. "You needed a birthday cake. It only came out of the vending machine, but they're usually pretty fresh." She held the plate close to Lily's face. "Make a wish and blow it out."

"That's sweet."

"I have an even better surprise. This package with a letter taped to the front came for you today." She pulled a chair to the side of the bed and held the package, wrapped in brown paper, close to Lily's face.

"Hand me my glasses, child. They're on top of my chest of drawers there."

"Look, it's printed right here on the front, 'OPEN ON YOUR BIRTHDAY.'" Sondra read the return address on the envelope. "It says it's from Jobie Greene, 635 Commercial Street, Provincetown, Massachusetts. That's way up north, isn't it? Is it from your granddaughter?"

Lily nodded. "Open the letter first and read it to me."

Sondra tore it open. "It says, *'Dear Mama, Happy 97th birthday. Clair and I are thinking about you tonight and wishing that we could be there in person to celebrate with you. Or even better, we wish you would come up here and stay with us. You're the reason we bought this big house in the first place.'*" Sondra put the letter down in her lap. "Miz Lily, you don't want to stay with your granddaughter?"

"No, I can't go way off up there, away from my people."

"But haven't your people mostly passed?"

"Yes, but I still feel them around me sometimes. They might not be able to find me up there."

Sondra sneaked a sideways look at Lily.

"Oh, honey, I'm just teasing you. Go ahead reading."

"'We're planning a trip to South Africa. The Travelers are playing a benefit concert in Cape Town.'

"Your granddaughter sings with The Travelers?"

"Her partner Clair does."

"'Deedee O'Gwinn is going with us to perform in Cape Town, too. I

don't know if you watched the Tony Awards, but Deedee was nominated again for Best Actress in a Musical, and this time she won! We're so excited for her. Proceeds from the Cape Town concert will go for providing better services in the shack settlements: water, electricity, sanitation. Can you imagine ten years after apartheid was abolished, and people still don't have bare necessities? I'll do some sketching while we're there for a show I'm doing this fall to raise awareness, and more importantly to raise money. Remember I used to be concerned about not having enough passion in my music? I finally feel I've found it in my art.

"'I love you and miss you every day, and I remember Papa and miss him, too. Please reconsider coming up to stay with us. We definitely plan to come down there for a visit after Cape Town.

"'Happy Birthday again. Jobie and Clair.'"

"Do you want me to open the package?"

"Yes, honey."

Sondra tore away the paper. "It's a painting. Oh, Miz Lily, it's beautiful."

She held up the canvas. It was an oil painting of a white, two-story clapboard house on a bluff above a beach dotted with sea oats. Two women stood on the front porch, their summer dresses fluttering in the breeze off the water. The one with silvery hair shaded her eyes and waved. The dark-haired one held open the screen door and beckoned the viewer to join them.

"Prop it up there on the top of the chest so I can see it."

"I'll get somebody to put it up on the wall tomorrow." Sondra held the picture at arm's length and studied it. "You should go and visit your granddaughter, Miz Lily."

"We'll see. I think I'll rest my eyes a little now, honey."

"All right, Miz Lily. I'll see you in the morning."

"Pull the door to, please."

Lily closed her eyes and listened to Jobyna's voice in the silence that settled around her.

About Jane Alden

Jane Alden was born and raised in a small Mississippi River Delta community in Arkansas. Everyone in town knew everyone else—their parents, and their grandparents before them. Though her father was a life-long cotton farmer, the family lived in town rather than on the farm, the only class difference in the all-white, all-protestant hamlet.

After graduating from the University of Arkansas, she moved to California and taught seventh grade English in a small central valley citrus-farming community. When she was recruited on the phone at U of A, she looked up Porterville, California, on the map, and it was only about an inch and a half north of Los Angeles, but it turned out the culture was closer to Arkansas or Oklahoma than to the bright lights and big city she craved. After two years teaching, she moved to Los Angeles and began a career in health care management. After many lucky circumstances and thanks to wonderful mentors, she ultimately became Chief Executive Officer at Los Angeles Children's Hospital, a mountain-top experience. After running a big organization for eight years, she became an executive coach, working with successful executives who want to be better leaders.

Jane and her partner of thirty years live in a small town thirty miles east of metropolitan Los Angeles. Claremont is rare for a Southern California town, having a distinct downtown village area and discernable city limits. Their chocolate lab, Delilah, is the captain of the domestic ship.

Visit Jane's website at janealden.com to chat about lesbian stories, our experiences, and other interesting things. 'Like" her on Facebook at Jane Alden, email Janealdenauthor@gmail.com. Connect with ...

Email: janealdenauthor@gmail.com
Twitter: @janealden5
Facebook: JaneAldenBooks
Website:

Note to Readers:

Thank you for reading a book from Desert Palm Press. We have made every effort to edit this book. However, typos do slip in. If you find an error in the text, please email lee@desertpalmpress.com so the issue can be corrected.

We appreciate you as a reader and want to ensure you enjoy the reading process. We would like you to consider posting a review on your preferred media sites and/or your blog or website.

For more information on upcoming releases, author interviews, contest, giveaways and more, please sign up for our newsletter and visit us as at Desert Palm Press: www.desertpalmpress.com and "Like" us on Facebook: Desert Palm Press.

Bright Blessings